RED GIRL, BLUE BOY

The  line

RED GIRL, BLUE BOY

An IF ONLY *novel*

Lauren Baratz-Logsted

BLOOMSBURY
NEW YORK   LONDON   OXFORD   NEW DELHI   SYDNEY

YA
Bar
c.3

First published in the United States of America in October 2015
by Bloomsbury Children's Books
www.bloomsbury.com

Bloomsbury is a registered trademark of Bloomsbury Publishing Plc

For information about permission to reproduce selections from this book, write to
Permissions, Bloomsbury Children's Books, 1385 Broadway, New York, New York 10018
Bloomsbury books may be purchased for business or promotional use. For information on bulk
purchases please contact Macmillan Corporate and Premium Sales Department at
specialmarkets@macmillan.com

Library of Congress Cataloging-in-Publication Data
Baratz-Logsted, Lauren.
Red girl, blue boy : an If only novel / by Lauren Baratz-Logsted.
pages   cm
Summary: As Katie's father and Drew's mother vie for the presidency, the sixteen-year-olds start—and
end—a romance, but the press finds out, both candidates' poll numbers rise, and the two are asked to
flaunt their former relationship.
ISBN 978-1-61963-685-9 (paperback) • ISBN 978-1-61963-500-5 (hardcover)
ISBN 978-1-61963-501-2 (e-book)
[1. Politics, Practical—Fiction. 2. Presidential candidates—Fiction. 3. Dating (Social customs)—
Fiction. 4. Celebrities—Fiction. 5. Family life—Connecticut—Fiction. 6. Connecticut—Fiction.]
I. Title.
PZ7.B22966Red 2015   [Fic]—dc23   2014032448

Book design by Amanda Bartlett
Typeset by Integra Software Services Pvt. Ltd.
Printed and bound in the U.S.A. by Thomson-Shore Inc., Dexter, Michigan
2 4 6 8 10 9 7 5 3 1 (paperback)
2 4 6 8 10 9 7 5 3 1 (hardcover)

All papers used by Bloomsbury Publishing, Inc., are natural, recyclable products
made from wood grown in well-managed forests. The manufacturing processes
conform to the environmental regulations of the country of origin.

For Lauren Catherine, aka L2, for a great decade of friendship and writing—here's to many more

BEFORE

12 YEARS AGO

The girl stood in the hot sun on a raised platform holding her father's hand. Her blond hair was in messy pigtails and she wore cutoff shorts revealing skinned knees. She had smudges on her cheeks and a few teeth missing. Green eyes shining, she briefly addressed the small group gathered round before looking directly at the video camera.

"A vote for Edward Willfield is . . ."

Most of the larger crowd was otherwise occupied at the outdoor festival, listening to musical groups under the band shell, getting their faces painted, buying balloons only to have them fly away, or eating fried dough.

Yet, there was something about the girl with the skinned knees and cutoff shorts that commanded attention and by the time she was finished with her brief remarks, two boys had joined the small group. As the others dispersed and the girl's father talked to a woman hanging out backstage with a clip-board, one of the boys approached the girl. He pointed at her knees.

"That looks like it hurts," he said.

She shrugged. "It's okay."

"When I skin my knees," the boy said, "my mom always puts Bactine on it."

"I don't have a mom anymore," the girl said.

"Oh, I'm sorry," the boy said.

"Me too," the girl said.

8 YEARS AGO

The boy looked at the picture of the girl in the newspaper. She was nothing like the girl with skinned knees he remembered from the festival a few years earlier. The girl in the picture had on a pink wool suit, even though she couldn't be any older than the boy, and her hair was swept up into a bun.

"Get the scissors," the boy said to his friend.

"What are you doing?" his friend asked after handing the boy the scissors he'd requested.

But the boy didn't answer, the tip of his tongue protruding slightly from the corner of his mouth as he snipped carefully.

When he was done, still gazing at the picture, he informed his friend, "Someday, she's gonna be my girlfriend."

"You're crazy!" His friend laughed.

"Maybe," the boy said. "But it's still gonna happen."

NOW

KATIE

I've been waiting for this moment forever.

Perhaps a PowerPoint presentation would best demonstrate what I'm trying to say. Picture a giant screen. First slide. A title card with the legend: "Katie Willfield's Political Life."

Here's me at four years old, the first time my father, Edward Willfield, ran for public office: I'm wearing shorts and—

You know what? Scratch that. I've got bigger fish to fry, plus, if I've played my cards right—and I'm sure I have—soon the whole world will want to know more about me. All you need to know about me right now is that I received my original clipboard, which I still have, and started helping my father with his first congressional campaign when I was four; wore my first pink Jackie O suit *and* made Katie Couric cry when I was eight (check it out on YouTube—thirty million hits!); and guided my father to strategic success in the Connecticut senatorial race when I was twelve, after which I was forced out of politics when a former campaign manager of my father's advised him that he should let me lead a normal life. Normal life? HA! Like I wanted that!

It's been four years since I was on national television, but tonight I'm finally going to be in the spotlight again.

My father is pacing the staging room nervously and I'm ticking items off my clipboard as Marvin enters; Marvin of the droopy eyes and handlebar mustache, my father's current campaign manager.

"Two minutes, Edward," Marvin informs him.

"I don't think I can do this," my father says. "In fact, I'm sure I *can't* do this."

I put my clipboard down, and take my father's hands in mine.

"Yes, you can," I say. "You say that every time, but you always come through." I pick up the clipboard and show him the remaining items on my list for today. "See? All that's left for you to do is go out with me at your side when they say your name. Then we stand there and wave to the crowd and let people clap for us. After a few minutes, when the clapping feels like it's reached its peak, we exit the stage and return to our hotel; we don't want to wait too long because if we wait until the applause starts dying, it looks like we don't know when to leave. And after that? You don't have to say another word! You can even go to sleep if you want to. In fact, you don't need to say anything else until your big acceptance speech tomorrow night."

My father's eyes look like he's about to go into panic mode again at that last sentence.

You'd think for a longtime politician like my father, giving speeches would be old hat, right? But here's something a lot of people don't realize. The number one, biggest fear people have isn't death—which is what you'd guess, right? It's public speaking. And even though most politicians don't experience that fear, running toward the thing most people run screaming from, my father has always had a bit of trouble with public speaking. Like some famous singer he once told me about from his generation who used to have panic attacks and literally get sick before each performance, my father has these brief moments of terror before giving speeches. And what could be more terrifying than this, the biggest political stage of all? Yet, he forces himself to overcome his fears each time—well, with a little help from me. And why does he put himself through this, when he's so wealthy from old family money that he could just lie around the house or play golf for the rest of his life? Because he believes that much in his message and ability to do good. As for me, I believe in my father.

"And when you give your big speech," I say soothingly now. "You'll be great. You always are."

As soon as I say the words, I see the fear fall away from him, just like it does every time. Right before my eyes, he transforms into the confident politician he needs to be.

By the way, the third biggest fear people have? It's spiders.

But there's no time for more soothing words because Marvin's giving me the nod, and as we hear the words over the loudspeaker, ". . . the Republican candidate for president, the next president of the United States, Edward Willfield," my father and I step out onto the stage, hands clasped, arms raised in triumph.

That's right. Because just like my father believes in his message and I believe in my father, the Republican Party now believes in him as well. A one-term senator from Connecticut, after a few terms in the House, seeking the highest office in the land? A fresh face in the crowd, coming out of nowhere to take his place in the political sun? It's like the Republican version of Obama.

I'm sixteen years old, and I've been waiting for this moment forever.

DREW

I've been dreading this moment for days.

I'm slouched in a chair, texting with my best friend, Sandy.

Him: Is this the coolest night of your life or what?
Me: Or what. This is definitely *or what*.

"Ahem." Suddenly, a dark blue suit is waved between my face and my phone screen. Ann. Of course.

Ann's my mom's campaign manager. She's all business, all the time.

"Come on, Drew," she says. "There's still time. It's exactly like the suit your brothers are wearing. You want to look like the rest of the family, don't you?"

I look over at my brothers, the twins, Matt and Max, who stand beside the Secret Service agent who's been assigned to them, Clint. Even though the twins are ten years younger than me, in their black suits and white shirts, skinny black ties, and slicked-back hair, they look like miniature Wall Street executives. Almost like they were born wearing those suits. But then, they practically were. They were just two years old when my dad made his fortune, so they don't even remember what life was like *before*.

Before was when my dad was a truck driver and we lived on the south side of Waterport, the poorest city in our small state of Connecticut. But then Dad went back to school and studied computers. Turns out, he is *really* good with computers.

I look down at what I'm wearing: the faded jeans, the work boots, the black T-shirt.

"Nah," I tell Ann with a smile, "I'm good."

"Did you see what Katie Willfield wore at the Republican Convention?" Ann presses.

"No," I say, which is a truthful answer. I didn't see her at the Republican Convention, because I didn't watch the Republican Convention. I did, however, see the picture on the front page of the *New York Times* the next day, her and her dad standing there with their joined hands held high. If pushed I'd have to admit that Katie Willfield was pretty with her blond hair and—what looked to be—green eyes; it was hard to be sure about the eye color, since the picture was one of those blurry ones. But that pink suit? Did she not realize that suit was an exact replica of the one worn by Jacqueline Kennedy, a Democratic icon? Let me say that again: a *Democratic* icon. Also, it was what Jacqueline Kennedy had on the day her husband was assassinated. So was Katie Willfield trying to be ironic or tasteless, or was she simply clueless?

Either way, that dress and those clasped hands raised in triumph: what a loser.

But there's something about that pink-suited loser. I've definitely seen her before. Maybe at the mall? Like an itch I can't reach to scratch, I just can't place her. And I have to admit, even in a blurry picture, she is cute. She's definitely got something going on there.

"How about doing it for your mom?" Ann just will not let this go. "Don't you think that, just this one night, you can make a little extra effort?"

Actually, no, I don't think I can, not even for just one night. Because I don't want this. I've never wanted this.

"Drew?" my dad says, tentatively, hopefully. "For your mom?"

I look at him. It's so hard to say no to him when he's looking all pathetic like that. He doesn't ask for much, not really. It's Ann who's always asking for things.

I'm a breath away from *maybe* giving in, when my mom speaks.

"You know what?" she says brightly. "It's fine. Really, Drew, it's fine."

Sometimes when a parent says, "It's fine," it's really the exact opposite of that and what it really means is "This is not fine at all, you are the biggest embarrassment who ever lived, I am just smiling through the heartbreak and pain, but that's okay, you do what you want, I'll just sit here and smile with the knife in my back."

But as I look at my mom closely and she continues to talk, I realize that for her, if not for Ann, this really is fine.

"Drew shouldn't change who he is just to conform to some traditional ideal," my mom informs Ann. "Besides, it's not such a bad idea to remind the voters of our humble Waterport roots."

Right. Our humble Waterport roots. Of course, we still live in Waterport, only now we're on the other side of the city, in the kind of fifty-room house and neighborhood no one ever thinks about when they think about Waterport.

Our roots may be humble, but almost nothing else about our life is anymore.

And all because my dad invented some little thing to do with computers that made him rich beyond most people's wildest dreams, after which he decided to use his newfound wealth to help my mom "follow her bliss" by entering politics. Some bliss. Our family is a campaign manager's fantasy. Certainly, we are Ann's fantasy: blue-collar roots and white-collar success, the American Dream.

To give my mom credit, when she first decided to run for president two years ago, because she believed she could make the kind of difference no other candidate could, she could tell I wasn't into it and she gave me the choice: if I was absolutely against it, she wouldn't run. But I could see it was something she wanted to do, so I told her it was okay as long as she kept me out of it. And even though it really hasn't been okay, for the most part, she has. Kept me out of it, that is.

Now that the suit emergency has been laid to rest, I go back to texting with Sandy.

I try telling him about the two things I'm looking forward to doing when I get back home: playing my electric guitar and working on the car. I love working on older cars and recently picked up a beauty of a clunker, a 1963 Corvair.

But tonight, Sandy doesn't want to talk about any of that. All Sandy wants to talk about is where I am.

Him: So, Atlanta. Hot-lanta. Met any hot chicks yet?

If only texting had sound. He would hear me scoff as I reply.

Me: *No*. Trust me, dude, this is all the opposite of fun. Political chicks are not hot.
Him: Can I tweet that? And attribute it to you?

Oh, the temptation. If I let him do that, maybe there will be a scandal and this whole ball of wax will start to disintegrate. I could get my old life back, or at least something resembling it.

But I can't do that to my mom. At least not tonight.

Me: No. Because if you did, Ann would blame you, you'd be banned from my life, and you would hate that.

And now here comes Ann again, only this time she's waving a pair of scissors.

What is *with* this woman? What does she *want*?

"There's still time for a trim, Drew," she says. "Come on; look at the twins' hair. Don't they look cute?"

"Yes," I admit, before adding with steely determination, *"but they're six."*

"How about a few inches, then?"

This woman just never gives up.

I finger my hair, which is a few inches past my shoulders. *Oh, why not?* I relent.

"Okay," I say, "but just one inch, because I need a trim anyway. But you take off more than an inch, and I am *not* going out on that stage."

Music is soaring, but it's not any music I'd ever care to listen to again, and the words come over the loudspeaker, ". . . the Democratic candidate for president, the next president of the United States, Samantha Reilly." My mom and dad walk out on the stage, waving to the crowd, with the twins sandwiched between them, everyone holding each other's hands, while I trail behind them, removed from the group.

I'm sixteen years old, and I've been dreading this moment for days.

KATIE

It's quite a thing, really, living in a town with the same name as a person, although I suspect I would feel differently if my name was Danbury and I lived in Danbury. Katie Danbury? It just doesn't sound right.

But Willfield? It's such a beautiful name, and such a beautiful town! All those houses in elegant styles—Victorian, Tudor, Greek Revival, McMansion—and almost all of them quite large. Plus all those sloping green lawns. I often wonder how anyone gets by with less than an acre of land. Even the weather is better here! We get fewer inches of snow in winter than the less coastal towns in the state do, and the proximity to water means that it's slightly cooler here in the dead of summer. Of course, too much rain or hurricanes can result in flooding. But hey, that's what insurance is for! Willfield even smells better than any other town.

I not only share my last name with the town, I also share it with the school I attend, Willfield Academy—well, of course! It was founded by one of my ancestors. (So was the town.)

I'm jolted from my daydreams by the groan of the Willfield Academy gates against the pavement as they open to let my limo through to school grounds. The limo drops me off in front of the main upper school building.

Willfield Academy, of course, has a ton of buildings: upper school, middle school, lower school, preschool, dining hall, field house, performing arts center, all of it on 150 acres of rolling lawns. Well, except for the sports fields; it'd be pretty silly if the soccer field rolled! Sometimes I'm astounded to think I've spent most of my life here—I've been here since preschool. Sometimes I'm even more astounded to think that soon, when I go to live in the White House, I'll be leaving all this behind.

"Have a good day, Miss Katie," Kent says.

"Thanks, Kent!" I tell my Secret Service agent. "See you after school!"

"I'll be waiting right here," Kent says.

This had been the source of some debate between my father and me, whether Kent should accompany me from class to class or just wait outside. I voted for class to class but my father thought outside was enough. He thought it would be too disruptive for me to have Kent with me every second, plus Willfield Academy does have very stringent security.

It's the first day back at school and I am, of course, wearing the school uniform: plaid skirt, white shirt, navy blazer. My tie is done in a tight full Windsor. Most of the kids wear their ties loose, and some even let the tails of their shirts hang out, but

I don't favor such a lackadaisical approach. If clothes make the man, they also make the girl, and you never know when cameras might be filming.

Oh, how I wish cameras were filming.

As I run lightly up the steps, a few kids call out, "Hey, Katie! Congratulations on your dad's win!"

I thank them as I sail on by, but inside I'm thinking: *Well, that's new and different.* No one's ever congratulated me on one of my father's wins before. Come to think of it, no one ever really talks to me, unless of course they have to, like if we're paired up in science lab or on the same volleyball team in gym. And even then, it's mostly just, "I'll put the drops on the slide while you record the results" or "Can't you hit the ball any harder?"

The truth is, I've never been what you'd call popular. It's not like anyone's specifically mean to me or anything, more like I'm just not one of the group. But that's okay. I totally get it. For twelve years, my life revolved around helping my father win one election after another, so it's not like I've had time to cultivate any friendships with kids my own age.

I know I said before that I was forced out of politics four years ago, but that was more in theory than in practice. My father's former campaign manager urged him to let me have a more normal life and he agreed—like I said, in theory. But in practice? It's impossible to keep a good woman—or girl!—down. Plus, politics is addicting. So I've kept on top of my father's campaigns and the polls, worked behind the scenes, and of course whenever my father has needed emotional support, I've been there for him. I just haven't been giving any more interviews to Katie Couric or otherwise basking in the limelight, that's all.

The bottom line is, it's not just that I'm not one of the group. I've never even had any friends at school.

From time to time, I'd tried to fit in when I was younger, but that never worked. I invited other kids to do things with me, only to have my overtures rebuffed. You might be surprised to learn that other kids don't find the prospect of being driven around in the back of a chauffeur-driven limo while playing what I *thought* was a rousing round of the License Plate Game to be particularly appealing. And I'd tried again in high school, only to be met with similar disastrous results. It's safe to say that kids my own age kind of scare me.

Every now and then this makes me sad, but mostly I'm okay with it. Once my father wins election to the highest office in the land, *then* I can have a life that has friends in it too. But until that day? Eye on the prize!

Still, it is nice having other kids congratulate me. It's actually nice just being talked to.

As the day continues, so do the congratulations. It makes me curious. If I had the time, I'd finance a poll so I could do a study on why there's been such a big change. But I don't have the time because I'm too busy rushing from class to class, meeting my new teachers, collecting assignments.

In fact, I'm getting a fresh notebook from my locker before heading off to Political Science—what a joke, me being required to take *that!*—when I sense a hovering presence. I look to my right and there's a boy there.

Now, that *is* new and different.

He's very tall, at least a foot taller than my 5 foot 2 inches. And although his tie is almost dangerously loose, the hem of his shirt is completely free of the waistband, and the crotch of his pants is hanging low enough to—well, I don't even know what to say about that—he is rather attractive. And the way he's leaning against the locker next to mine and staring at me, I get the feeling he's waiting for something.

"Can I help you?" I say.

"Yeah, listen, Katie, I was wondering: would you like to go out with me this Friday night?"

I almost drop my fresh notebook.

I'm about to say yes. After all, I've never had a boyfriend before; no one's ever even asked me out on a date before! But then a thought occurs to me and I tilt my head to one side. "Do I know you?"

He looks surprised. "I'm Jayson. I'm the captain of the basketball team."

"Oh. Well. Good for you." I pat him on the arm. "Sure, I'll go out with you Friday, but I have to get to class now."

Inside, I'm dying. In a few days, I'm going on my first date!

"Great," Jayson says. "I'll walk you."

As I walk toward Political Science, my notebook clutched against my chest, he falls into step beside me. That's when it hits me: *he's walking me to class.*

Hold the campaign-donation phones.

I think I have a boyfriend!

• • •

As others head into Political Science, Jayson stops me by putting his hand on my elbow. Then he leans against the wall near the doorway. I must admit, he does seem rather big on leaning. But once we settle more deeply into couplehood, I'll be able to change that.

"So listen, Katie," he says, "I was wondering."

Suddenly he seems nervous, which is odd. He didn't seem nervous when he asked me out on a date. What could be harder than that? Oh, gosh. Is he going to ask me to go *steady* . . . *already*?

If I was prone to internal screeching, I'd be doing that right now.

"Yes, Jayson?" I say, helping him along.

"Um, do you think your dad could get me courtside tickets to the Knicks when the season starts?"

"What? Why would he do that?"

"It's just that, I've seen presidents at games before. I know that, like, when a guy is president, he can get tickets to whatever he wants to see. *Really good* tickets. So I just figured . . ."

"Oh, no, Jayson." I shake my head sympathetically. *What a ninny*. Then I explain. "He couldn't do that. Using his power and influence to do favors for friends—that would be unethical, not to mention a gross misuse of taxpayer funds."

"Oh." He looks puzzled. "Oh, yeah."

My Political Science teacher, Mr. Snowden, shoots an impatient pair of raised eyebrows in my general direction as he holds the door.

"I've really got to go now," I say. "So, what time on Friday?"

"Yeah, about that. I just remembered, I don't think I can do this Friday."

And he stops leaning and moves off.

Wow, that's it?

That was a whirlwind relationship.

Oh, well. I shrug as I enter Political Science. I'll be heading off to Washington in a few months anyway, so really it was a doomed romance from the start.

When I get home from an otherwise typical first day of school, I grab some carrot sticks from the fridge and put them on a plate with some chocolate chip cookies. Then I tuck a water bottle under one arm, pick up the plate, scoop up my white Himalayan cat, Dog, with my other arm, and head up to my room.

My room is my own pink-and-white palace. Every now and then, it occurs to me that I should update the decor, make it a more sophisticated color. But Dog and I like it, no one else ever really sees it except for my father and the maid, and anyway, we'll be moving to Washington soon.

I sit down at the chair in front of my computer, position Dog on the tufted cushion beside me, and boot up.

Immediately, I go to "The Kat and Dog Blog."

It's something Dog and I started years ago. I've always wished people would call me Kat, but no one ever does. Everyone just calls me Katie. Well, except for my father, who calls me Kathryn sometimes, but only when he's mad at me.

On The Kat and Dog Blog, we simply post whatever strikes our fancy that day. I might say to Dog, "Do you think our readers would be interested in learning more about the Magna Carta?" And then Dog will either curl up in my lap, which I interpret as a yes, or start licking himself, indicating that he thinks the day's topic is a snoozer. But it doesn't really matter. It's not like anyone ever reads it. I've never had a single comment. In fact, whenever I check StatCounter daily, it appears that the only hits I get are from people who stumble onto the blog by accident, people who want to know the answers to questions like: "What do I do when my cat and dog try to kill each other?" Thankfully, Dog and I don't have that problem.

I originally started the blog because I read an article in the *Times* about how it's an activity some teens like to do. In the beginning, I thought I should tell my father and his people about it—you know, in case they had any objections—but like I said, no one ever reads it anyway.

"So," I ask Dog, "what should we write about today?"

There's a knock at the door.

"Yes?" I call out, turning in my chair as my father opens the door and walks in.

"How was your first day back at school?" he asks.

Sometimes, he acts so much like a regular dad, it's tough to remember that soon he'll be the Leader of the Free World.

"It was good," I say, "different." I'm about to tell him about my whirlwind relationship with Jayson, but as he perches on the edge of my bed, I notice he looks nervous. Odd. I seem to be having that effect on males today.

"What's up?" I ask.

"Look, I know I promised I wasn't going to ask you to do any more campaigning for me—"

"A promise I never asked for," I cut in.

"—and I know I said I wanted you to have a normal teen life, but . . ."

My excitement starts to grow. "Dad," I say, trying not to appear too eager, "what are you saying?"

Maybe Marvin's out as my father's political adviser and I'm back in?

"It's just that Marvin said he got a request today from one of the morning talk shows," my dad says.

Oh. Marvin's still in.

"You know how they're always looking for new angles," my father says.

Don't I know it. The 24-hour-a-day news beast must be fed.

"Well," my father says, "they've been going on and on for the past few weeks about how this is the first time since 1944 that both major-party candidates have hailed from the same state."

"Right," I say. "In 1944, it was Franklin Roosevelt and Thomas Dewey, both from New York."

"Exactly. Well, they've kind of beat that into the ground, at least for the time being. So now, apparently they've seized on the fact that both Samantha Reilly and I have kids in high school who are exactly the same age."

That doesn't seem that newsworthy to me. Still, if there's a chance I'll get on television again . . .

"So what do they want?" I ask.

"They want to do a joint interview with you and Drew Reilly tomorrow, maybe even a series of interviews. You know who Drew Reilly is, don't you?"

Well, of *course* I know who Drew Reilly is. I saw the pictures in the *New York Times* after the Democratic Convention. There was the Reilly family, Samantha and the First Man Wannabe and their little twins looking all spiffy and presidential-hopeful. Not that that will do them any good. If wishes were horses, everyone would ride—well, except for people who are scared of horses. And then there was Drew hanging in the background, looking all slouchy and removed. A good-looking slouchy and removed, but still. And even if I hadn't seen that picture, based on the progression of this conversation, sheer logic would tell me who Drew Reilly is.

Actually, there's something annoyingly familiar about him, like maybe I've met him somewhere before.

But who cares about that right now, because . . .

"Of course I'll do it!" I fly at my father to give him a big hug. "And they want to do it tomorrow?"

"Yes. But what about you having a normal teenage life?" he asks, hugging me back.

That's the funny thing about my father. He doesn't seem to ever notice that whether I'm officially helping his campaign or unofficially working behind the scenes, my teenage life is as far from normal as can be.

"Oh, *pfft*," I reassure him quickly before he talks himself out of this, "I'll still have that. You know I love our life." I may have gone all nonchalant on the outside, but internally I'm clapping quietly. Yippee! I get to go to a green room again! "It's just one interview," I reassure him some more, "maybe a series. What harm can it do?"

With my father gone, Dog and I return to The Kat and Dog Blog.

I'm so happy about this latest development, it's tough to think about what to write on the blog today. I mean, I *could* write about the interview coming up tomorrow, but I don't want to jinx it. So I go on yet another virtual tour of the White House and before long, inspiration strikes.

I realize that for state dinners, we'll need to use the china with the presidential seal on it. But what about other events? What about every day?

"Dog," I say, clicking on Google Images, "let's find some pictures of china patterns."

Several hours later, I'm in bed for the night, Dog curled up at my side.

Before turning out the light, I look at the framed portrait on my nightstand. It's a picture of me when I was three years old, sitting in my mother's lap. It was taken right before she died. I wish I could really remember her.

There are two mes. There's the version I think of as the regular-print me, the one who lives out loud, for public consumption. And then there's the other version, the one I think of as the small-print me, the part that no one else ever gets to see, unless you include Dog.

Small-print me misses my mom even if I can't really remember her. Small-print me sometimes wishes that my life was more normal and that I was more like other people, that I went on dates and felt a part of things.

And sometimes, small-print me gets lonely.

DREW

The bus picks me up at the bottom of our driveway. It was a long walk. It's a long driveway.

The driver smirks at me as I trudge up the steps. "Can't you just take the limo?" he says.

I ignore him. The twins take the limo, accompanied by Clint, to their private school but I still ride the bus to mine. Even after my dad struck it rich, I insisted on going to the same public schools I would have in the old neighborhood. Of course, it's not the same. In my old neighborhood, kids hung out together outside all the time, talking, playing sports, just hanging. Then we moved here and it's like you can't even see the next house. Plus, everyone just stays inside all the time.

My mom taught me when I was very young, "Drew, popularity doesn't matter. If you have just one good friend in this life, you've got it made." Of course it would be rich if she tried to say this to me now, the woman trying to court every vote in the country, hoping to win the biggest popularity contest America's got going. Still, it was good advice to give a little kid and I've lived by that advice. I have Sandy. Even if he teases me mercilessly sometimes, and I him, we've been through thick and thin together, through poverty (ours), wealth (mine), sickness and health, and I still know that we'll always have each other's backs until the day one of us croaks.

All my other friends from the old neighborhood? Once my family had money, they changed. People liked me more because I had it or they resented me because I had it. And then there were the times, if I'd complain about something, I'd overhear other people muttering, "I wish I had his problems." That's the thing you learn fast when you have money: no matter how bad things get, you're not allowed to have problems. The only one who didn't change the way he acted around me was Sandy.

So do I need anyone else? For the most part, no.

I'm the only kid in my neighborhood who takes the bus, so I make the bus driver unhappy because he has to go all out of the way of his route just for me. But hey, that's his problem. I feel like saying, "We pay taxes too, you know," but instead just make my way down the aisle to an open seat. Along the way, a few girls shout congratulations on my mom getting the nomination, but I just nod, plop down, put in my earbuds, and zone out by the window.

Soon the mansions disappear, replaced by seedier and seedier houses as we progress. Eventually, we hit Sandy's neighborhood, a bunch of kids pile on, and in a second Sandy's next to me.

"Dude," he says, "I tried to text you last night but your phone's not working."

"Yeah, you're going to have to use the landline from now on."

"The landline? What are you, *nuts*?"

"Actually, it's your fault."

"*My* fault?"

I explain to him that my mom is usually pretty cool about things, but after Sandy tweeted my comments to him from the convention center (which I told Sandy not to tweet) and Insta-grammed the pictures I sent him of me slouched in my chair looking bored, right before going onstage (which I also told Sandy were just for him), there was a resulting mini-scandal ("Democratic Nominee's Oldest Too Cool for Glory") . . . so my mom decided it was time for me and modern technology to part ways.

(Yeah, I know that's a really long sentence with—count them—three parenthetical asides, but trust me, my mom's side of the discussion was even longer and she didn't even pause for breath.)

"She says it's for my own good," I say, "to protect me, just until after the election."

"Harsh," Sandy says. Then he considers before adding, "Sheesh. If I'd known this was going to happen, I would've posted something juicier."

• • •

The first day back at school is always such a strange animal, with things either dragging or zooming by too quickly, sometimes at the same time. After what feels like a week, and yet almost before I know it, Sandy and I are at lunch.

I'm examining my burger for large, hard things—wouldn't be the first time I've found something—when the bench I'm sitting on bounces. I look to my left and there's Millicent Carraway.

"Hey," I say as I take a huge bite of burger, having concluded it's safe enough to eat.

"Drew," she says, hand trailing up my arm, "I'm having a little party on Friday."

"Good for you," I say. Another bite.

"Would you like to come?" she says. "As my date?"

"That's awfully nice of you," I say, "but thanks, no."

The entire table grows quiet. What happened? Did I speak in a foreign tongue?

"Okay," she says, recovering her smile as she rises, "but if you change your mind . . . *when* you change your mind . . ."

"I won't, but really, thanks for the offer. I'm good."

She's barely out of earshot before Sandy starts hissing at my other side.

"No? Thanks for the offer? *I'm good?* Are you out of your mind?"

Sandy may be talking to me, but he's watching Millicent walk away. I have to admit: that long black hair, those practically sprayed-on clothes—she sure is something to watch.

I shrug it off.

"That's been happening all day," I say.

"What? Hot chicks throwing themselves at you?"

Another shrug. "Pretty much."

"And you just keep saying, what, *No, thank you*?"

"They're just doing it because of my mom. They think it's cool she got nominated. They think it's cool she might be president."

"So?"

"It's not real."

"*So?*"

"When I go out with a girl, I want it to be real."

"Oh, man." I can feel Sandy's disgust. "You are one sick puppy."

After school, I'm barely through the door when Ann pounces and starts pulling me through the kitchen.

Do I get to eat a snack first? No.

Do I even get a chance to say hello to my father first? No. My dad is just one openmouthed blur as Ann zips me by. I swear, no matter how this campaign turns out, I'll be glad when it's over just to get Ann away from me.

"What gives?" I say as Ann practically drags me into my mom's study. "I didn't do anything. I didn't even touch anyone else's cell phone."

"It's not that," my mom says.

Then Ann starts in on some whole dog-and-pony show about some morning news program; about how they've been obsessed with the two-candidates-from-the-same-state-who-live-in-neighboring-towns angle for the past few weeks; about how now they've become obsessed with something else. And that something else involves me.

"You've got to be kidding me," I say to my mom. "You want to exploit me on national television?"

My mom winces. "It's not like that."

"If you ask me, it sounds exactly like that. A live interview? *Tomorrow?* You said if I was okay with you running, you'd leave me out of things."

"Drew, don't you think you're—" Ann starts in. But for once, my mom cuts her off.

"I know I said that," my mom says, "and I meant it. But tomorrow I leave for a midwestern tour. The poll numbers are just so close: up one day, down the next. Sometimes even the most minor thing helps. So if, just this once, you could see your way clear to . . ."

Her voice trails off. It kind of hurts to see her looking so concerned. And a part of me would like to see that Katie Willfield up close, to see just how green her eyes are when not slightly obscured in a blurry picture. Still.

"Yeah," I say. "*No.*"

KATIE

I'm in the green room of the New York studio of *That Morning Show*, Kent waiting just outside the door, set to go on in fifteen minutes. It took just eighty minutes to drive here and now I'm waiting to be interviewed on national television—yippee!—and I'm wondering where the boy is. Shouldn't he be here by now? But then I think: Maybe he's so casual, with all that slouching, he's waiting until the last second to stroll in? Or, perhaps *That Morning Show* is worried that, with us being political enemies and all, we'd scratch each other's eyes out if we were left in the same room alone together. So they're keeping him somewhere other than the green room.

The green room, for those not in the know, is never actually that color, which is a good thing today. Given that I'm wearing a red suit, if it were that color, it'd look like Christmas in here. Although I'm still worried I'll remind people too much of Christmas due to my green eyes.

Actually, no one knows for sure why the room where performers wait to go onstage or interviewers wait to go on camera is called the green room. So naturally, there's been a lot of wild speculation on the term's origin over the past several decades. Some think it's a corruption of "scene room." Some think it has to do with Shakespeare referring to the stage as "this green plot." Some think it goes all the way back to the Blackfriars Theatre in 1599, and that room really was green!

As you can see, there's been a lot written on the subject—far more than I've detailed here—and I've read all of it, because I'm nothing if not professional and in the know about all things related to the political process. Particularly interviews. (Also? Dog and I did a blog post about it once.)

Actually, being professional is why I'm wearing a red suit today. I'd been planning on wearing my trademark pink suit, but then a curious thing happened. I got an e-mail late last night through the contact form on The Kat and Dog Blog. I was so excited to see it there—my very first fan e-mail . . . ever!

Then I read it.

Dear Kat: You really need to stop wearing that pink Jackie O suit. Don't you realize, she was a Democrat and you're a Republican? Also, that she had on that suit the day her husband was assassinated? When you look at it like that, don't you think it's kind of offensive?

Offensive? I never meant to *offend* anybody. No matter what Jacqueline Onassis's political affiliation, she was an American treasure and a fashion trendsetter. I'd only ever meant it as an homage!

The fan e-mail, which had turned out to be sadly wanting on the "fan" part, was unsigned but it did contain a P.S.:

P.S.: And picking out the china patterns? Dude, isn't that a bit premature?

I suppose I should have been offended at being addressed as "Dude." But I'm aware it is a term implying friendly familiarity in the vernacular of the modern America teen, so truth be told, I was kind of flattered. It was almost as good as the long desired salutation of "Kat"!

As for the rest of the e-mail, I must admit it stung a bit. Still, despite the sting, I am nothing if not capable of learning from my mistakes, making changes as situations require. Hence, the red suit.

I am *always* a professional.

And because I'm a professional, even though I'm tempted by the array of culinary goodies available in the green room—oh, mini muffins!—I staunchly resist. Because as any professional will tell you, you do *not* eat any food in the green room right before going on camera. Afterward, maybe. But before? Can you imagine getting the opportunity to be on national television, but then your entire message gets lost because people can't stop focusing on the *food* stuck in your front teeth? That would be—

"Miss Willfield?" The speaker is some kind of casually attired stagehand with a headset and clipboard. "We're ready for you now."

"Great!" I put on my second brightest smile. Might as well save my brightest for the actual show.

I follow the stagehand onto the set and am introduced to George Gibson, one of the cohosts of *That Morning Show*. I'm glad it's him and not his cohost. Everyone in America loves George Gibson. He's such a good listener and always looks like he'd be so easy to talk to. But I feel inexplicable dismay as I'm invited to take a seat, he takes his, and I realize these are the only two seats currently on the set.

"But where's the boy going to sit?" I blurt out.

I've been so looking forward to meeting my enemy—er, political counterpart—face-to-face. I know I could take him! Not to mention, if I'm being honest, it would be nice being part of a conversation with someone close to my age, however adversarial that conversation might get. Besides, the boy really *is* cute. There's still something so . . . *familiar* about him. I just can't put my finger on it yet.

But no one answers my question. All I hear is the countdown from the cameraman until airtime.

"And we're live in five, four, three, two, one!"

"We're here today with Katie Willfield," George addresses his introductory comments directly into the camera, "the only child of presidential hopeful and junior senator from the state of Connecticut, Edward Willfield." George turns to me. "Katie, how are you this morning?"

"I'm great, George!" I know to address my answers directly to him, resisting the temptation of the amateur, which is to look directly into the camera. It should appear to the audience like we're just two friends chatting. Still, I can't resist asking my new friend George, "But where's the boy?"

"The boy?" George echoes.

"Yes. Where's the boy going to sit?"

George just looks at me. Well, I suppose that just because he gets twenty million dollars a year for coanchoring a morning show, he's not necessarily a Harvard rocket scientist.

"The boy," I prompt. "You know, candidate Reilly's son?"

I know I should be focusing on my father's political agenda right now, but somehow the boy's absence really bothers me.

"Oh!" And . . . *bingo*. The light of comprehension finally illuminates George's eyes. "For some reason, he couldn't make it today."

"HA!" I can't help myself. "What a wimp!"

"Excuse me?"

Why is he having trouble comprehending?

"I'm sorry, George. Do I have the lingo wrong? When I tried to master the Urban Dictionary, in order to enhance my grasp of current teenage slang, the definition for the word 'wimp' was given as 'a person who is scared or weak or cowardly.' Is that not right? And if candidate Reilly's son refuses to meet with me in a place as safe as your show—I mean, it's not exactly the Romans in the Coliseum—doesn't that make him a wimp?"

I'm not sure why I'm being like this. Why is it so important to me that the boy be here? It's possible that I somehow feel rejected that he didn't even bother to show up. But that would just be silly. I shrug it off.

"Um, I believe he declined to appear today," George says. "You know, Katie, that's a lovely suit."

"Oh!" Suddenly I feel flustered. "Thank you."

"With your green eyes, it kind of makes me think of Christmas."

Well, shoot.

It takes me a moment to recover from realizing the boy is a no-show and even longer to recover from George's Christmas crack, but I'm a professional. Besides, George immediately moves to sharing photographs of my life with the viewers at home and asking me questions. I'm on more certain ground here. In fact, I knew it was coming. Prior to agreeing to the interview, my father had Marvin insist that we be allowed to see the questions in advance. The show tried to balk at this ("Where would the spontaneity be?") but Marvin held firm ("She's still a minor and we don't want you taking advantage. There'll be no blindsiding. If we can't preapprove the questions, no interview.").

At the time, I kind of resented the implication that I could be blindsided, but now I'm grateful for the predictability.

The first picture George shares is one of me when I was four years old. I'm wearing shorts and my knees are skinned. This is back before I gave up soccer and took to wearing power suits all the time. I've got a few teeth missing and there are smudges on my cheeks as I stare directly at the camera.

"So," George says, "talk us through this photo, Katie."

"It's a still photo from a campaign ad I made during a stop with my father in his first run for public office. In the commercial,

I said, 'A vote for Edward Willfield is a vote for your future. Please elect my daddy to the United States Congress.'"

"Very nice."

"Of course, when I saw the commercials playing on TV, I became appalled. My father's campaign manager at the time, Sissy Bertucci, would never appear in public dressed like that. Sissy was the only woman in my life back then."

"Your mother died the year before, when you were three, right?"

"That's right, George. She died of cancer. And I still miss her, even though I only have pictures to remember her by. Sissy impressed me as being everything a woman should be: smart, perky, organized. When, shortly before the next election, Sissy eloped to Hawaii with an envelope-licker, I saw my chance and leaped. *I* would become my father's new campaign manager. Well, technically, Marvin has that title. But I knew my father would need someone else in his life to help organize things. That's when I got my first clipboard."

"A clipboard?"

"Oh, yes. Sure, I can do a PowerPoint presentation like nobody's business, and I've got an iPhone, an iPad, and anything else *i* to come down the pike, but nothing can replace a good solid clipboard when a person's on the campaign trail."

"Okay," George says, "what about this shot?"

It's the one of me at age eight, wearing the first of what would become my trademark pink wool Jackie O suit with matching pumps. Yikes. I wish when I'd gotten that fan e-mail last night, I'd thought to have Marvin call up the network to remove this photo. But, no point in dwelling on that now—I've got to power on.

"That was taken during one of my father's later congressional campaigns, George. I'm being interviewed by Katie Couric on national television. You can't see her in this shot, but by the time the interview was over, *she* was the one with tears in her eyes. Really, though, had I known saying that I wished I could remember my own mother better and thought she, Katie, was brave for having raised her kids on her own was going to make her cry so hard, I might have dialed it down a notch. I don't know what brand of mascara the makeup department on her show uses, but whatever she had on that day, it was *not* waterproof."

"And viewers can still find that interview on YouTube."

"That's right, George. Thirty million hits!"

"Finally," George says, "this last shot?"

It's me at age twelve, again with the pink Jackie O suit. Yikes!

I could tell George so much about this picture, considering it represented the beginning of my ousting from political life.

There was a recession, a depression, inflation, deflation, stagnation, and pretty much every other "-ation" going on at the time. Okay, maybe all those things can't go on at the same time, but the economy had definitely gone cablooey. And even if there was only one of those -ations, there was also confrontation, in the form of Corbin Cox III, who challenged my father for a seat in the US Senate.

The race was too close, scarily close. People wanted change. The people of Connecticut wanted change and they didn't care what form it took, even if that form was Corbin Cox III, who kept saying insulting things about my father.

"Just take it," I had counseled my father at the time.

"Are you crazy, kid?" Marvin said. "The press'll eat him alive."

"No, they won't," I countered, steely as I held my clipboard close to my chest. "If Cox keeps throwing stones, Dad gets to take the higher ground. He gets to say things like, 'I don't believe in negative campaigning' and 'If my esteemed colleague chooses to spend his time engaging in schoolyard mudslinging, I respect his right to do so. But if it's all the same to you, I think I'll spend my time serving the best interests of the Nutmeg State.'"

For the record, I do a very credible impersonation of my father. Very basso. *Very* profundo.

Marvin looked skeptical. "I don't know, kid. You really think the best strategy for your dad is to just, basically, lie there and take it?"

It was all I could do not to roll my eyes.

Okay, I did roll my eyes.

"Have you never seen *The Godfather*?" I said with a world-weary sigh.

"About thirty, forty years ago. Why? What's *The Godfather* got to do with anything?"

"Sonny's brother-in-law. The only reason Sonny's henchmen don't kill the brother-in-law outright for laying a hand on Sonny's sister is because the brother-in-law just lies there and takes it."

I didn't add the part about the brother-in-law getting killed later on. Why poke holes in my own argument? Anyway, by the end of *The Godfather* almost everyone else is dead too, so it's not like any one strategy ever saves anyone forever.

"I still don't know," Marvin said. "Edward, what do you think?"

My father cocked his thumb and forefinger and pointed at me. "Gotta go with the kid, Marvin," he said. "She's never steered me wrong yet."

My father made the right decision. He listened to me and we won the election, even if it was a squeaker.

A year later my father got a message from Sissy in Hawaii. Sissy wasn't getting in touch to say she wanted back in. Rather, she wanted me out. She said she'd been seeing me on too many political TV shows and now that I was entering my "important teen years," I should be allowed to retire from the limelight. She said it was too much pressure for a kid my age and that I should just be allowed to have a "normal life."

If it were up to me, I would have told her to mind her own business.

But it wasn't up to me. My father cut me off, cold turkey. He said Sissy was right. He'd taken advantage of me long enough. Taken advantage of me? His campaigns were my life! So my father relented. He said I could help with strategy, if it was that important to me, but I was to give no more interviews, either print or on TV. He didn't want me subjected to that kind of scrutiny.

At the time I was tempted to say, "Ex-*cuse* me? Where would you be if I hadn't made Katie Couric cry and if I hadn't known so much about *The Godfather*?"

Still, a good politician knows when the only road to success is compromise. I could tell that, just this once, if I pressed my father for more I'd wind up with less. So what else could I do? I caved.

Four years later, I'm back.

I always knew it was just a matter of time.

But I don't tell George any of this because even though everyone understands that everything to do with politics is Machiavellian, at least on some level, no one wants their nose pressed in it. And when you're a politician, even a politician's daughter, you *never* publicly cite *The Godfather* as inspiration for your campaign. I mean, who else will they blame if horses' heads start showing up in people's beds?

So, I do the only thing I can do. I tell George, "Um, that's just a picture from my father's senatorial campaign."

"I see," George says. "Well, that's all the time we have. Our thanks to Katie Willfield." Then he leans a little closer toward me, real intimate, and I wonder if this is like at the end of *The Daily Show*, when the host bestows the special handshake of friendship upon favored guests.

But there is no special handshake.

"Oh, by the way," George confides, "I love the china pattern you picked out."

"China pattern?"

"On The Kat and Dog Blog, for when you're in the White House. The Kat and Dog Blog—that's you, right?"

And . . . *CUT!*

DREW

There's one film that everyone in the world has seen and can agree is the greatest movie ever made.

I'm not talking about old classics like *Gone with the Wind* or *Citizen Kane* or more modern Best Picture winners like—heaven forbid—*Titanic*. (Like movies are supposed to be great and we're all supposed to be so sad when the hero dies in the end? Jack didn't have to *die*. He was strong, he could've pulled himself up on that floating door too. That door would've held both of them!) And I'm certainly not talking about *The King's Speech*. (We're supposed to feel so bad for the guy? So what if he had an impediment—he was still king!)

I'm talking about *How the Grinch Stole Christmas*. And I don't mean the Jim Carrey abomination either. No, I mean the 1966 version, with Boris Karloff doing the Grinch's voice as well as the narration.

Okay, so I'm talking about a cartoon.

Let's call it a twenty-six-minute animated feature made for TV.

Anyway, am I not right? *Everyone* has seen *The Grinch* and everyone *loves The Grinch*. Even Jatheists, like Sandy. Sandy's father is a Puerto Rican Catholic and his mother is Jewish. Sandy leans toward his mom but questions the existence of God, explaining the reason why he refers to himself as a Jatheist. If you ask me, he could just as easily call himself a Catheist but that doesn't sound as cool—it sounds like he's pro catheters or something. Not like that'd be something a person would be anti. Also, since he questions the existence of God, he should really refer to himself as a Jagnostic, but that doesn't sound as cool as Jatheist either. Anyway, from a young age, my mom taught me not to question anyone else's religion. Or lack thereof.

Of course it was Sandy, the Jatheist, who first got me started watching *The Grinch*. We were five and having a sleepover at his place close to the holidays and it was on TV. He'd seen it the year before and wanted to watch it again. I swear, near the end, I looked over at him and there were tears in his eyes. We still watch it together annually and he still cries every time. I've never said anything to him—why embarrass the guy?—but part of that could be that even if I'm not actually tearing up myself, I do get a lump in my throat.

And you know what that's like, right? Because it probably happens to you too. It happens to everyone.

Sandy always starts to get teary when the Grinch is heading back up Mount Crumpit with all his ill-gotten Who booty. Morning has arrived and he has Max the Dog stop the sleigh. He knows that the Whos will all be waking up, discovering that Christmas has been stolen from them, and he can't wait to hear the sounds of them weeping.

Only he doesn't hear that at all.

The Whos hum, their humming starting out low but steadily growing in joy and resilience to a fever pitch, a crescendo of sheer goodness that almost can't be believed. Then the Whos sing that crazy indecipherable little Who song, their voices soaring up the snowy mountain. (I mean, really. "Fahoo fores"—what is that?)

And the Grinch realizes that no matter what he's done, he couldn't steal Christmas.

It's a killer emotional moment—gets me every time.

So, this? What I'm about to tell you about? It's exactly like that.

It starts out low and begins to grow.

There's just one difference.

In my case? It's not about anything good.

It starts out low.

I'm at my locker, getting my books for first period. I hear a voice call my name, turn around, and who do I see but Millicent Carraway walking by. I start to say the usual "Hey, how's it going?" but there's something in her smile as she opens her mouth that stops me. She leans closer, mutters a word, and it's only when she's gone that the word penetrates my shocked brain.

Did she just call me a wimp?

No, that can't be it.

But when I search my mind for possible alternate words that rhyme—"limp, primp, pimp"—none seem to apply, nor are particularly reassuring.

Maybe she called me a chimp?

I shrug it off.

So yeah, it started out low, but then it began to grow.

And it's a little harder to shrug off a short while later when I'm in English class. We just finished reading *The Book Thief* last night and now Ms. Parmalee, the teacher, is asking all kinds of questions. At first, they're just your basic opinion questions, the kinds of things there's no real right or wrong answer to. Like, did you find the characters believable? Or, *did* you like the writing style? Or, would you read another book by this author? People raise their hands like crazy to answer those questions. It's like those lame participation trophies given out just for good attendance or for being on an athletic team, no matter the team's ratio of wins to losses. I hate those trophies. It's like sending a message that simply showing up is enough. Like it's an accomplishment to be physically there, even if you don't actually do anything, or even if your team sucks.

So yeah, people raise their hands, falling all over each other to answer these dinky questions, because they know they'll get credit for class participation, even if their answers are stupid or totally off the wall, like when Tom Meeker says, "I would absolutely read another book by this author, but only if he writes one involving a lot of *cats*."

But then, as inevitably happens, the dinky questions move to thinking questions. Also inevitably, hands stop going up. This means that Ms. Parmalee, rather than waiting for volunteers, will call on helpless victims instead.

"Drew?" she says. "Can *you* tell us what the effect is of the mystery surrounding Max's life after his reunion with Liesel after the end of the war?"

I read the book and what she's asking doesn't even make sense to me. She must steal these questions, clearly designed for maximum confusing wordage that might trip kids up, from some kind of online guide for teachers. There's no way she's making all of this up on her own so early in the day.

But that's the thing. It *is* early in the day. And I am *not* a morning person. In fact, I'm more of the kind of person who thinks all students would achieve more if the school day started a few hours later. And maybe ended a few hours earlier. So *maybe* if she had asked me this question after ten in the morning—better still, after lunch—I might have something for her. But as it is, all I can do is shrug and say: "I got nothing."

And *that's* when Susie Fallow—shy Susie Fallow, whom I haven't heard say a single word to another human being since like third grade—pokes me in the shoulder with her eraser and mutters the word, "Wimp."

I spin in my seat and Sandy, seated beside me, spins too.

"Did Susie just—" Sandy starts to say.

But he never gets a chance to finish, because now the second word I've heard from Susie's mouth in eight years comes flowing out:

"Scared."

And a third: "Weak."

And a fourth: "Coward."

Followed, finally, by a vehement return to the first: *"Wimp."*

Oh, man. Something's definitely going on here.

KATIE

Once I recovered from the shock of having George ask me about my china pattern, I realized I would have loved to discuss it with him. I'm sure George wouldn't have minded since we both have excellent taste. But by the time I did, the interview was over, I was being whisked offstage, and that was that.

Oh, the things a person wishes she could do over again. If I could, not only would I discuss my china pattern, I'd also ask George, "Just who does Samantha Reilly think she is? An out-of-nowhere candidate with no previous political experience?"

To which George might counter, "Well, Ross Perot was just an American businessman, and he ran in 1992 and 1996."

To which I'd counter, "Right. But that was on an Independent ticket."

To which George might counter, "But there've been others who've run for the major party nominations in the past."

To which I'd counter, "Like who? Herman Cain? The God-father's *Pizza* guy? And just because some have run for the nomination, it's not like any of them got it."

To which George might counter, "But this time, one has. Polls show the American people are increasingly tired of the same-old same-old in politics. They don't want Washington insiders, they want an outsider, making Samantha Reilly the perfect populist choice."

Okay, come to think of it. I'm glad we didn't have *that* discussion.

As soon as I'm out of the glare of the set, I check my phone and see that I have one text. It's from my father:

Katie, there's something we need to discuss.

Even though we're aware that it's common practice to text in abbreviations, my father is firmly against it. He always says that full sentences are what sets us apart from lesser animals—well, that and opposable thumbs—a sentiment with which I wholeheartedly agree. So I text back in kind:

What about?

I wait for his reply expectantly, my excitement growing. He's probably so impressed with how I handled being on national television, he wants me to be a more front-and-center participant in his campaign. Maybe he'll even send me out to stump for him in Iowa.

But when his reply comes back, there's no mention of Iowa at all. In fact, it's downright cryptic:

It can wait until after school. But as soon as you get home, come see me.

Hmm . . . that's perplexing.

Oh, well. I shrug it off as Kent holds the door for me and I climb into the back of the limo with a sigh. I sigh because while a few people have taken phone snaps of me, there is no real press in sight to mark my progress. Did I mention that I blame Bill Clinton for this? Here's why:

Once upon a time, the sitting president's children were fair game for the press. Those children were considered public property, much in the same way that the offspring of the royal family in England still are. Why, Tricia Nixon was even married at the White House in 1971 in a ceremony that was aired on national television. (So romantic. If a person's going to ever get married, could there be anything more romantic than a White House wedding?) And don't get me started on poor little Amy Carter! Poor little Amy Carter was mercilessly ridiculed by late-night comedians—I'm looking at you, *SNL*! But then along came Bill Clinton. He and Hillary basically said, "Take all the cheap shots at us you want to, but leave the kid alone. We're the public figures here but she's not. She's just a kid who didn't ask for any of this. Let her be a kid." Chelsea was twelve at the time her father was elected and the press listened. They attacked Bill and Hillary at every turn, but wonder of wonders, they left Chelsea pretty much alone.

True, the Bush girls later came under some heat, but they were nineteen when their father was elected, and therefore practically adults. But the Clintons? They set the template that the minor children of presidents should not come under close public scrutiny, not unless they invite the press and cameras in, a precedent that the Obama children were later the beneficiaries of. Was there ever anything in the press about Sasha and Malia, except for the occasional pictures of them on vacation wearing incredibly cute clothes? If there was, I don't remember it.

So like I say, this is all Bill Clinton's fault. Because while maybe Chelsea and the Obama girls were happy flying under the radar, being allowed to live as normal lives as possible while their fathers were serving the greater good, I'd love a little public scrutiny. I'd love a little more limelight.

We start heading back toward Connecticut when a thought occurs to me.

"Kent," I say, "do you think we could stop somewhere for a Cronut?"

It's been hours since I ate my earlier-than-usual breakfast and, remembering the array of goodies I passed up in the green room, I'm suddenly famished.

"Sure thing, Miss Katie."

• • •

School.

With my early morning appearance on *That Morning Show* today, my father told me in advance that if I wanted to, I could just skip the whole day of school. After all, what would be the point anyway of going to school when I will have already missed several periods of classes? But I told him that I wanted to go. I said that I felt it was important for me to get in as much class time as possible since, with campaign season heating up, who knew how many days of classes I might miss this fall? (Of course, I've made arrangements with the school, so I can keep up with assignments no matter what else is going on.) Plus, once he wins and we're in the White House, come January Willfield Academy will be behind me forever. If he's president for just four years—which I don't see happening—I'll be in college. And if he's a two-term president, which of course he will be, I'll be twenty-four, a college graduate, possibly a grad school graduate, maybe even a PhD. Maybe I'll even be married! Well, probably not that. As soon as I graduate from college, I'll probably go into politics like my father.

Anyway, that's what I told my father: that I didn't want to skip school today because I couldn't bear to miss these last days at Willfield Academy.

But really?

I'm here for the accolades.

Even in a school as exclusive as Willfield Academy—where everyone's families are wealthy, where everyone's parents are some form of a professional big shot—being on national television is still a *very* big deal. We boast not one but four Olympic hopefuls and we have pep rallies for them regularly. There's Harold Chu, who plays table tennis; Carol Zabriski, who does air pistol/air rifle; Janice Jacobs, who competes in something called eventing (it's some horse thing); and Jim Stevens for racewalking. Of course, none of these are exactly edge-of-your-seat, must-see marquis events like gymnastics or ice skating. Have you ever tried to watch racewalking? After thirty seconds, it's like, "Time to reach for the remote." I mean, what can you say about it? "Ooh, look at those elbows go"? But at the moment, those are our hopefuls. In addition to them, we also have a TV star, Marly Simpson. Actually, she's an ex-TV star, which I think is kind of sad. At the height of her self-titled Disney Channel show's popularity, Marly was easily the most popular girl in school. But then she grew eight inches in a single year, became too tall to play age thirteen anymore and lost her cute "kid" look, and her show got canceled. The part I think is sad is that her popularity sank like a stone. If people liked her when she was on top, they should have liked her the same when she was not. I don't think Marly's ever gotten over it.

That's one thing I've always appreciated about my own lack of popularity: at least it's a constant.

But yesterday, it was announced during morning assembly that I was going to be on *That Morning Show* today, so I'm sure people will be congratulating me right and left like they always do when any of the other students guest star on a TV show or win an Olympic medal or something. Of course, I won't be stupid or naive about it like Marly. I know their flattering words will just be their flattering words, and instant popularity doesn't really mean anything. No matter what happens, I'll remain the same levelheaded girl I've always been. Still, I just *know* there will be a river of accolades flowing my way.

And as I open the door to Willfield Academy, that's what I'm excitedly thinking:

River of accolades, take me away!

Huh. Well, that was strange.

Because forget a little stream of accolades . . . There's not even a trickle.

It's as if I was never even on the show. Did no one see it? Was my segment canceled and I wasn't told about it?

There's only one tiny drop and it comes at the end of the very last class of the day, Political Science. I'm leaving the room when Mr. Snowden stops me with: "Katie, nice job on *That Morning Show* this morning."

I know I said that success wasn't going to change me, but the truth is, the absence of any kind words about my accomplishment has stung a bit. So it's gratifying to finally have this acknowledgment, however meager.

"Why, thank you, Mr. Snowden," I say, modestly lowering my eyes as my mood brightens.

Which is when Mr. Snowden chuckles and says, "But china patterns? Have your people learned nothing from Nancy Reagan?"

Now, what does *that* mean?

DREW

"Wimp" and words similar to it follow me through the morning and lunch. But it's not until gym class—another thing about school that I would change, like, who is happy running around right after eating really bad food?—that the chorus rises in fever pitch to its crescendo. Only, unlike in *The Grinch*, that crescendo is the opposite of sheer goodness.

We're playing volleyball, which in itself is stupid. I mean, come on, volleyball? It's like this lame combination of tennis and basketball only without a circular net.

When it takes me two serves to get the ball successfully over the net, I hear, "Weak." When I—graciously, I might add—allow the person next to me to take an easy shot, I hear "Coward" and "Scared." And when the person on my own team—my team!—nails me square in the middle of the back with a serve, I hear everyone in the gym except for Coach

Grigson, say a resounding "*Wimp.*" Hey, I may not care much about what other people think of me, but this is starting to get physically abusive!

And yet the only thing Coach Grigson says after I flinch at the force of the hit is "Reilly, stop clowning around."

What? I feel like telling him "Hey, Coach, why don't you just go back in your office and smoke one of those illegal-to-smoke-in-school cigarettes you've got there."

But of course I don't. I ignore him. I ignore everything . . . until it becomes impossible not to.

But when a second server on my team nails me square in the back with a serve that's even harder than the first one was, I whirl in place and see Millicent standing there, a smirk on her face as she unmistakably mouths: Wimp.

That's it.

Now I know what's going on here.

Ignoring Coach Grigson's shouts—all some variation on "Get back in your own position, Reilly!"—I close the small space between me and Millicent, grab her by the upper arm and whisper-hiss, "Seriously, Millicent? You're doing all *this* because I said I wouldn't go out with you? I mean, I know that maybe I might have hurt your feelings and all, but I always thought that, underneath it all, we were kind of friends."

The reason I whisper my hisses? It's because, even though I'm madder at her than I have been at anybody in I don't know how long, if I talk louder, other people would hear. And a public declaration that I turned her down would likely embarrass her. And even though she maybe has it coming to her, for spreading who knows what kind of made-up smack about me, I can't bring myself to do that to her because I know what public embarrassment feels like. It's what I feel like right now. It's what I've been feeling all day.

But Millicent does something surprising.

Instead of looking—what's the vocab word?—*chastened* that I'm onto her little scheme, she *laughs*.

Right in my face.

"You think *this* is about *that*?" she says, and may I add, she does nothing to keep her own voice to a whisper. On the contrary, she speaks so loudly, it's obvious she doesn't care who hears what she's got to say to me.

"You think," she continues, "that this is some kind of lame payback just because you were stupid enough to say no to me?"

"Well, yeah," I say. I mean, isn't the answer right there in the hostility of her own question?

"Don't flatter yourself," she scoffs.

"Then what?" I demand.

"Do I have to spell it out for you? Katie. Willfield."

What?

It takes me a moment to realize who she's talking about: that little pink-suit-wearing First Daughter wannabe. Which makes no sense.

"What???"

In books, the phrase "and then she rolled her eyes" has always struck me as being extremely over the top. I mean, like, in real life, who does such a thing? But right then, Millicent does it. She rolls her eyes at me.

"Need more spelling out, Drew?" Millicent says with a weary sigh. "Fine. I'll help you out here." And then she enunciates three words: "*That. Morning. Show.*"

I'm still in the dark, which gives Millicent time to lay on one more zinger: "Nobody likes a wimp, Drew. You're a disgrace to this school."

I open my mouth to respond, but it turns out Millicent has three final words for me: "Look it up."

For the rest of the day, I handle things by doing what I pretty much always do: ignore all the sound and fury around me. (I got that sound-and-fury thing from Shakespeare.) I go to my classes, keep my head down, and ignore the taunts.

But then on the bus ride home, after I tell him the cryptic things Millicent said, Sandy makes me realize that this is not a quo I should allow to become my status.

"If nothing else, dude," Sandy says, "we have to find out what she's talking about."

"I have to admit," I say, "at this point, I am morbidly curious."

He pulls out his iPhone.

"So let's look it up," he suggests.

"Not here," I say.

In the way of best friends, without having to explain, he immediately understands. Whatever this . . . *thing* is, I can't find out about it in a place populated by the cruelest group of creatures known to man: a crowded bus of high school students.

So we agree that Sandy will call his parents to say he'll be a little late and instead of getting off the bus at his house, he'll wait for mine. His parents can come pick him up later.

The first thing we do when we get to my house is hit the Sub-Zero fridge for something to eat so we can fortify ourselves. After studying the contents, Sandy finally settles on the leftovers from last night's dinner: something called lobster thermidor.

As soon as I remove the plastic-wrap covering, my dog, Bowser, comes running, toenails scratching eagerly at the kitchen floor, excited at the smell. "Don't you remember what happened last time?" I say, holding it out of reach. "Sorry, boy, it's too rich for you. No way am I cleaning up that mess again."

Once we retire to my bedroom—or should I say, my bedroom *suite*, complete with my own bathroom and sitting room—and shut the door, officially corralling it off as a dog-free zone, Sandy pops a large chunk of lobster into his mouth. Before he even swallows, he says, "Is it okay for me to say that I like coming over to your house better now that you're rich than I did when you were still poor?"

I pick up a chunk of lobster and chuck it at him.

"Yeah," Sandy says, looking around, "definitely better rich than poor."

"Yeah," I admit, "I suppose the extra space is all right."

In the old house, I had to share a room with the twins and one bathroom with everybody.

When Sandy pulls out his iPhone, I move to my desk and turn on my computer with a screen bigger than the TV in our old house.

"You won't get in trouble with your mom for this?" Sandy says.

As if on cue, the twins open and fill the doorway. Or at least fill it as well as pint-size six-year-olds can. Behind them hovers their Secret Service agent, Clint. All three have on dark sunglasses. Inside.

"Mom says you're not supposed to be online," Max says.

"I'm telling Mom!" Matt says.

Matt is frequently the more annoying of the two.

"I can't use my iPhone." I sigh. "But I can still use my computer. I need it for school, don't I?"

"Oh," Max says.

"Well, okay," Matt says, "but if you use your iPhone, I'm telling Mom!"

And they're gone.

"Nitwits," I mutter under my breath. This muttering-under-your-breath thing can be pretty contagious.

"Is that true?" Sandy asks. "You can still use your computer?"

"Of course," I say. "Only they track my history and they've disabled IM. Also, they monitor my e-mail."

"Dude, when your mom is prez, she's already going to have all that covert surveillance stuff down pat."

I grin ruefully. "I know, right?" But of course, my mom being prez—I don't have to worry about that, or about my life changing at all, because it's never going to happen.

In the end, it's as easy as looking up *That Morning Show* on YouTube and plugging "Katie Willfield" into search.

And there she is, frozen on my big screen in all her red-suited glory.

"You gotta admit," Sandy says, "she looks pretty hot in that thing. Maybe a little bit Christmassy, but still."

I chuck an eraser at him. Sandy's got a thing for females in suits. Don't even get him started on our chemistry teacher when she's wearing her lab coat.

I have to admit though: Katie does look pretty cute in that suit. At least, it's definitely an improvement on that stupid pink one that I have an annoying and confusing affection for.

I click on the picture. Might as well get this show rolling.

We watch as the cohost, George Gibson, greets Katie and she greets him back. Then she asks, "But where's the boy?" And that's soon followed by, "Where's the boy going to sit?"

I pause the screen.

Sandy hits me in the shoulder with the back of his hand. "Dude! She's talking about you!"

"I know," I say. "But I told my mom I wasn't going to do the show. How come no one told Katie?" And why does she seem so concerned about my whereabouts?

I click the screen to continue and George does tell Katie I'm not coming.

And that's when she delivers the diss heard round the world—or at least the world of my school. She labels me a wimp, going on to define the word, courtesy of the Urban Dictionary, as "scared, weak, cowardly." And then she adds some insane stuff about Romans in the Coliseum. I'd really like to reach through the screen and tell her: the Romans fed the Christians to the lions in the Coliseum, so they were just there as *spectators*!

"I can't believe she'd do that after I tried to help—" I start to say and then stop myself.

"Help what?" Sandy says.

But I just shake my head. I can't tell Sandy that the other day I used his phone to send Katie an anonymous e-mail through that ridiculous blog of hers, warning her against wearing that pink suit. I mean, someone had to tell her, right?

We watch the rest of the interview in mute horror: not because of anything she says—the rest of the interview is a little self-involved but otherwise it's fine since none of it involves me—but rather, mute and horrified about what she's already *said*.

"Dude," Sandy says when it's over, "like, what are you going to do?"

"Dude," I say back, "like, nothing."

"Nothing? Are you *crazy*?"

"What do you expect me to do—punch her in the nose?"

I've never hit a girl before. I've never hit *anyone* before.

"Of course not," Sandy says. "Look, I understand. You like to turn the other cheek. It's who you are. I get that about you, I've always got that, I've even admired it. But that won't work this time. You can't let this stand."

"Sure I can. I'll just ignore it, pretend it never happened. I don't care what anyone else thinks about me except you. And if I ignore it, won't it just go away?"

"No," Sandy says. "I don't think so. Didn't you see Millicent and the others today? It's like chum in the water, man. It's like freaking *Jaws*. No way is anyone in school going to let this go. You got to nip this thing in the bud. We're talking about your reputation here."

"I don't care about my reputation."

"Fine." Sandy pauses. "Then we're talking about your *honor*."

The thing about a really good best friend, one who's known you your whole life, is that while they know exactly what to say to make you feel better, they also know exactly which button to push when you need motivation to get you to do the thing you need to do.

It's like something in my head explodes. I'm out of the chair, racing through the house and searching for my mom, Sandy hot on my heels.

With a fifty-room house, we're actually racing and searching for quite some time. Yeah, I did say fifty rooms. I know. The place is like a small palace.

Finally, we find her in the last place she ever is these days: the kitchen.

"Drew—oh, hi, Sandy—did you eat the rest of the lobster thermidor?"

I ignore her question, particularly since, you know, I know she won't be happy with my answer.

"I need you to call *That Morning Show*," I say.

"I thought you didn't want to go on there?" she says, puzzled.

"Well, now I do."

"Fine, I'll have Ann make the call."

"Good. Also, you need to call"—I practically choke on the name of that wool-suited little twit; no girl, no *person* has ever annoyed me more—"Katie Willfield."

"I can't call up the sixteen-year-old daughter of my opponent, Drew. It's simply not done."

"Fine. Then have Ann call her or have Ann call 'her people'"—I nauseate myself by doing the air-quotes thing—"and get her back on that program same time as me."

"Of course, Drew. But what's this all about?"

Now I'm so mad, I windmill my arm like a pitcher, jabbing my forefinger in the air as I declare, "I will *not* have my honor besmirched!"

Followed by a second windmill, which is accompanied by the gauntlet-throw-down words, "I will *meet* that little Roman in the Coliseum!"

KATIE

I'm relieved to be back in the limo and heading for home. Now that this uneventful day is over, I just want to put it behind me. But no sooner does Kent close the door than I pull out my phone to check for messages. And no sooner do I do *that*, than I see my father's text from earlier in the day. Immediately, I again begin to speculate what he wants to talk to me about. At first I'm excited, thinking that surely this must mean he wants me to play a more prominent public role in his campaign.

But then, remembering how wrong I've been about other things today—expecting the boy to be there, expecting a river of accolades just to wind up with only that strange remark from Mr. Snowden—I begin to worry: What if I'm wrong about this too?

Being wrong about three things in a single day—I don't think that's ever happened to me before but I suppose anything is possible.

But if I am wrong again, then what does my father want to talk to me about? And what if it's . . . something bad?

I rack my brains, trying to think of what it could be. But it's a short racking.

In fact, the only thing I can come up with is me calling that Drew boy a wimp on TV.

I groan and hit myself in the forehead—but not too hard.

That's *got* to be it.

"Dad," I say, holding Dog under one arm and holding up the other hand like a traffic cop to stop him from speaking after I find him in his office. I ignore Marvin lurking like a depressed mustachioed gnome in the corner of the room. "I know *exactly* what you're going to say. Insulting the opposition—what a rookie mistake! If my hands weren't otherwise occupied right now, I would hit myself in the head."

"That's not—"

"I know I used to tell you that mudslinging wasn't for us, that if anyone was going to sling the mud, let the other man or woman do it. We'd be above all that. And then there I go, calling that Drew person a wimp. How could I have been so stupid? If you think it best, I'll grit my teeth and issue a public apology. In my defense, though, I was thrown by his not being there. Now, if someone had informed me in advance—"

"That's not it, Katie."

"Then what?" I search my brain. "It *can't* be because when George Gibson showed that last picture of me, I failed to elaborate on the context. I know my answer was a little thin, but I also know that we agreed long ago to never publicly discuss using *The Godfather* for campaign strategy."

"It's not that either, Katie."

"Then *what?*" I don't usually get so flustered or exasperated with my father, but I'm at a complete loss here.

"It's this."

He turns his open laptop around so I can see what he was looking at when I walked in.

"Oh!" I say, surprised and delighted. "My china pattern!"

But delight soon turns to dismay when I see the stern look on my father's face.

"Don't you like it?" I say. "I personally think the band of gold is quite elegant. And if you're worried about the floral pattern"—I point at the screen, adding reassuringly—"those flowers are so tiny, I don't think anyone could accuse you of being insufficiently masculine over *that*."

"The pattern is not a problem, in and of itself," Marvin puts in.

"Then what is, Dad?" I say, ignoring Marvin once again.

"*That Morning Show* must have researched you online before your appearance and came across this previously obscure . . . *blog* of yours. That's why George Gibson made that remark to you about the china pattern. Of course, since they agreed to only ask questions from a preapproved list, he couldn't ask you about it directly."

"Ohh-*kay* . . ." I still don't see where this is going.

"But after you left the set? In the next segment? They displayed this picture from your blog for all of America to see."

"They *did*?"

"Oh, yes. They even gave the name of your blog, The Kat and Dog Blog."

"They *did*?"

"Oh, yes," he says again.

But this is amazing—what great press! I'm tempted to ask my father if I can use his computer to check StatCounter. My stats must finally be through the roof! But something in his expression stops me.

"And?" I ask cautiously.

"And then," he says, "they brought up Nancy Reagan."

Huh. Mr. Snowden also referenced Nancy Reagan. How odd—you don't think of a person for years and then suddenly they're everywhere.

"You do know who Nancy Reagan is, don't you?" my father prompts when I fail to respond.

"Well, of course!" I say with a laugh. "Nancy Reagan was the wife of the late Ronald Reagan, the fortieth president of the United States. Nancy Reagan is a Republican icon!"

"Nancy Reagan was also famously skewered in the press for ordering four thousand, three hundred and seventy-two pieces of very expensive Lenox china."

"Did you look that figure up on Wikipedia, Dad?"

"That's hardly the point!"

"No," I admit ruefully, "I suppose not."

"Even though the china wasn't paid for with taxpayer money—it was privately funded—the public, through the press, was certainly led to believe it was. People were outraged. Over two hundred thousand dollars for a few plates?"

"Well," I say in the former First Lady's defense, "I think four thousand, three hundred and seventy-two qualifies as a few more than a few—"

"Again, Katie, not really the point!" My father sighs. "What do people say when they want to criticize a candidate for jumping the gun on his own election? Come on, Katie. This is Politics 101."

I look down at my red shoes, humiliated. "They say he's already picking out the wallpaper and the drapes." Then I look up defiantly, meet his eyes dead on. "But I didn't pick out any drapes."

"For the last time, Katie, not really the point here!" Another sigh. "The last thing, the *very* last thing we want to ever do here is *hand deliver* ammunition to the other side. Do we want them saying, 'Look at Edward Willfield! He's already picking out the china!?'"

"But it wasn't you, it was m—"

"*Katie*," he warns.

More looking at my shoes. "No, sir. Not the point."

"All right, then."

I look up in time to see him also looking at my shoes and then he gestures at my whole outfit, adding, "And it didn't help matters any that you're wearing . . . *that*."

"What's wrong with my outfit?" I liked this suit so much when I first picked it out. Am I about to hear another Christmas crack again?

"Nancy Reagan was known for wearing little red suits, just like that."

Dawning realization. "Oh." Then: "But we're Republicans. It's like our team color."

"Still, between that and the china pattern pictures on your blog . . ."

"Do you really think lots of people looked at the blog today?" I ask.

My father snorts. "It'd probably be easier to count how many Americans *didn't* look at it!"

Oh, how I'd love to get my itchy finger on that Stat-Counter!

"The press is going to have a field day," my father says.

"What do we do?" I really want to help now. "Do you want me to make a public apology? Because I'd be happy to grovel, throw myself on my sword, tell everyone how it was all just me—so silly!—and how you never knew anything about this at all."

"I'm afraid that won't be enough, Katie."

"Then what will?" Wait, is he planning to exile me, like Napoleon on Elba? Maybe I'm overreacting but political history is not kind to those in power who make mistakes.

"You need to take down The Kat and Dog Blog."

Wait. What?

"What?"

"Make it like it never existed," my father continues, oblivious to my outrage. "Obviously, people will have taken screenshots and what have you, so the current damage from this can't be changed. However, we *can* minimize any additional damage going forward."

"But," I object, embarrassed at the smallness of my own voice as I look down at Dog, still tucked under my arm, "what will Dog and I do for fun without The Kat and Dog Blog?"

"I don't know, but you'll have to think of something. What I do know is that, clearly, you can't be trusted online. Which reminds me." He holds out his palm. "I'll need your iPhone."

"*What?* Why?"

"After the trouble that candidate Reilly's son got into texting his friend rude comments from the Democratic National Convention, I read a story about his mother taking away his iPhone. Samantha Reilly may be my opponent but I have to say she can be a smart woman, and in this, she was one step ahead of me." He snaps the fingers of his waiting hand. "Phone please, Katie?"

Grudgingly, I reach into the pocket of my suit and surrender the requested item.

Great. Now how will I stay connected to my father's campaign? Check poll numbers, opinion pieces, or what political pundits are saying?

"Great," my father says.

At least one of us is happy.

"We'll get through this," my father says, smiling for the first time since I walked in here, a real politician's smile. "We always do. But we can't afford to give them any more ammunition. *We* need to stay one step ahead of *them*."

"Yes, sir."

I turn with Dog, preparing to exit.

"We can't afford to make any more mistakes!" he calls after me.

Dog and I trudge up the long winding staircase to our pink fortress of solitude. I flop down on the bed, Dog beside me. We look each other in the eye.

"Great," I tell Dog glumly. "Now what do we do?"

But I am nothing if not resilient. Sadness turns to anger as it occurs to me: this is all that stupid Drew boy's fault!

Okay, maybe not the whole thing with the china pattern—I did that to myself.

But me losing my iPhone? That is *totally* his fault. If he hadn't gotten in trouble first, and if his mom hadn't thought to take away his iPhone, my father would *never* have come up with the idea to take away mine, not on his own.

Come to think of it, the whole problem with the china? *That's* that Drew boy's fault too! If he'd shown up for the interview—*like he was supposed to*—George Gibson would have had *two* of us to interview. Why, the interview segment would have filled up so quickly, George would never have had time to bring up china patterns.

So this is all *definitely* his fault.

I've never been so mad at anyone in my life.

And I've never even talked to the boy!

I knew that Drew person was trouble from the first time I saw him slouching on the front page of the *New York Times*.

I can't believe I let myself get so obsessed with him on *That Morning Show*.

Stupid boy. Stupid show.

I may be mad at He Who Shall Not Currently Be Named, but I'm not mad at my father—he's only doing whatever he needs to do to get us where we want to be: the White House (small yippee!). Still, I know when it's best to lie low, avoid the line of fire, fly under the radar—and a whole bunch of other military metaphors.

I don't go down for dinner. I have Cook send my meal up and I stay in my room quietly studying, only going on the Internet when I absolutely have to for homework.

I've been up since three in the morning to prep before my trip into the city, so by nine p.m. I'm ready for bed.

I'm already tucked in, wearing my pink satin Oriental pajamas, when there's a knock at the door.

"Katie?" My father pokes his head around the corner. "Can I come in?"

I reach to turn the bedside light back on and sit up in bed.

"So, listen," he starts, looking a bit nervous.

And, as he proceeds to talk, I think: Wait a second—he's here to give me my phone back! That *must* be it. He's going to apologize for being so harsh with me earlier and then he's going to return my phone. Yippee! Then I think: Poor Dad. All these years of trying to be both dad and mom to me. It hasn't been easy on him. He's certainly made his share of mistakes but he sure has tried. Finally I think: Hey, am I going to get my blog back *too*?

The problem with all this thinking is that I totally miss everything my father says, right up until I'm yanked back to reality by the following words penetrating my brain:

"—so obviously I need you to go on *That Morning Show* again."

"Wait. What? After telling me you want me to stay away from my iPhone, the Internet, and the media, you want me to go back there again? But why?"

"Katie." My father sighs. "Do we need to get you tested for ADD again?"

"Just explain again. I was preoccupied before."

"Short version this time: Samantha Reilly's people called our people. Apparently her son has decided that he would like to go on *That Morning Show* after all . . . and he wants to go on with *you*."

Small-print me thinks: The boy wants to go on the show now . . . with *me*?

"And you're okay with this?" I say.

My father shrugs. "What choice do we have? If we refuse, *we* look like the wimps this time and like we've got something to hide."

Even though I can't see myself in a mirror right now, I know my eyes are gleaming as I clench my fist and say, "Yes! I *know* I can take that kid."

"This isn't about 'taking' anybody, Katie," my father cautions.

"It's not?"

"Of course not. As a matter of fact, I think it would be a good idea for you to apologize for the rude things you said about him."

Not so much gleam anymore. "Do I have to?"

"I'm afraid you do."

Rats.

"I expect you to take the high road. I expect you to be polite to him at all times."

Double rats.

I have to apologize to my mortal enemy . . . *and* be polite?

"Still, if the opportunity presents itself," my father continues, "I know you'll show your superior political savvy and fitness to be in the White House in every way."

Yes! And back to pumping the fist.

In fact, I'm so encouraged by his last words, I dare to dream out loud:

"If I'm going back on TV, does this mean that I get my phone back? And my blog?"

"Of course not!" My father roars with laughter. "Don't be absurd!" But he adds, "Maybe after we win the White House." And then he's gone.

Briefly, I think: Who's really putting up the drapes and picking out the china pattern here? Which one of us is really putting the political cart before the horse?

But all of that is swept from my mind as I remember everything I've lost today and all because of one person, one person I'm now going to have to *apologize* to and be *nice* to on national television.

I can't stand that Drew boy.

Really, I can't.

DREW

So, like, you know how sometimes you get these . . . *preconceptions* about people? You've seen the person around, you've heard stuff about them, maybe you've even heard them talk a bit, and you think, Wow! What a jerk! But then you actually get to finally *meet* the person, face-to-face, and you realize that everything you thought about the person before was just so wrong, and you think, Hey! You're not so bad after all!

Well, let me be the one to . . . *disabuse* you of that notion as I say to you:

HAHAHAHAHAHA*HA*!

No.

Just, no.

• • •

I ride Metro-North into the city, listening to my iPod and playing with my younger brothers' Game Boy because they're the only devices I'm allowed to use now when I'm out of the house.

When my mom's "people" set up this joint interview through Edward Willfield's "people," she said she wanted me to take a car and driver for protection but I told her that was whack.

"No one's going to bother me, Mom," I said. "You're the famous one. Me? I'm like the most . . . *nondescript* teenager in the world."

And it's true. As I ride the train in, attired in jeans, a plaid flannel work shirt over a T-shirt, and a skateboarding beanie—Ann tried to get me to wear a suit but I resisted, although I do have a wool tie in my pocket that I promised to put on before going on camera—no one bothers me at all. No one even looks at me. Of course, that may be because everyone else on Metro-North this insanely early in the morning is some kind of suit-wearing executive, with a nose pressed to the financial sections of the *Wall Street Journal* or the *New York Times*, but still. No one knows me, no one recognizes me, and I like this just fine.

As we pull into Grand Central Station, I think: let's just get this puppy over with.

I make my way through Grand Central Station, with its zodiac constellations soaring overhead, stopping just long enough to grab a fat turkey sandwich at Junior's and a large coffee at Starbucks to consume on my walk to the TV studio. I ate breakfast just a few hours ago—bacon, eggs, toast, pancakes, more bacon—but that's worn off already. Hey, a guy's got to eat.

As I near the studio, I see a huge crowd milling around outside the building. I've got a few minutes before I *absolutely* have to check in, so I stand on the fringes of the crowd, chewing on my sandwich, waiting to see what all the fuss is about. I notice that the crowd is a mixture of all ages, including people my own age. I find this surprising since, like, shouldn't they be getting ready for school? Has something happened? Are people waiting for someone famous? A rock star? An actress? I try to see but, ah, I got nothing.

I tap the shoulder of the guy standing closest to me, who looks to be in his twenties.

"Dude," I say when he turns, "what's with the crowd? Like, what's everyone waiting for?"

"*Dude,*" he says back, with I might add, an unhealthy level of sarcasm, "we're here because of *That Morning Show?*"

"That's cool, because I'm supposed to be on—" But I never get to finish what I was going to say, because the guy just continues with, like, an attitude.

"You have heard of *That Morning Show*, haven't you?"

"As a matter of fact—"

"Every weekday morning, a crowd stands around—locals, tourists, people from all over the world—waiting for one of the stars to come out, hoping to get on camera."

I look around me and for the first time I notice that many of the people are holding homemade placards that say things like "Kalamazoo loves you, Joe!" and the ever-popular "Hi, Mom!"

Can you say "lame"?

Suddenly, a roar goes up from the crowd. The guy I've been talking to goes up on his toes, craning his neck to try to see over the heads of the people in front of us, and I do the same. I manage to see a microphone flash and glimpse about a quarter, maybe from the eyebrows up, of some guy's head. I hear a jovial laugh coming from the general direction of the microphone and now the crowd is really going, with shouts coming from all over the place, including from my new friend, each some version of, "Hey, Joe! Over here!"

I tap the guy on the shoulder one more time and he turns.

"Yes?" he asks impatiently.

"Who's Joe?" I say, popping the last bite of Junior's turkey into my mouth.

"Are you *kidding* me?" He looks at me like I'm insane. "Joe *Schwartz*? Like, only the most famous weatherman in the country, maybe the world?"

Wait. These people are all standing here at this insane hour, they do this every day, hoping for a glimpse of—or better yet—some kind of deep personal exchange . . . with a weatherman?

My companion waves a dismissive hand at me, before firmly turning his back on me. Correct me if I'm wrong, but I have the sneaking feeling this conversation is over with.

What am I even doing here?

Indeed.

My instructions say that rather than going through the front entrance, there should be a side door for guests. When I locate it, I find a second crowd outside of that and I have to kind of force my way through to get to the front. A burly man with a walkie-talkie stops me as I try to enter, but after I give him the song and dance about who I am and why I'm there, he calls upstairs and lets me right on through.

I hear some muttered variations on "Who's that?" as the door opens for me, but I ignore them. I put the earbuds of my iPod back in, switching on my Game Boy as I stroll toward the elevator.

For about the millionth time since I woke up this morning, I curse the name of Katie Willfield.

If it weren't for that screwy girl, I wouldn't have to go through all of this.

Another guy with a walkie-talkie meets me at the elevator and escorts me up. When I step off, there's a woman with yet another walkie-talkie who leads me to a door.

"Here's the green room," she says. "You'll wait here until your segment is called."

The green room is decidedly not green. It's also empty of other people. So I take a seat on the couch, and focus on my Game Boy, hoping to just kill some time until I can get this thing over with. I'm just sitting there minding my own business, listening to some tunes, when one of my earbuds is rudely yanked from my ear. I look up and there she is:

Katie Willfield.

The cause of so much trouble in my life. She's everything I can't stand about just, well, everything. But up close like this, I see that she's just a girl. And, surprisingly pretty. The suits she wears may make her look stuck-up, but at least the one she has on today is green, which matches her eyes. At least she's not wearing the red one, or worse still, the pink one. Suddenly, *confusingly*, I feel the anger flush out of my body.

"Hey," I say mildly, "how's it going?"

I don't know what I'm expecting. Maybe "Nice to finally meet you"? Or your basic, "Fine, how's it going with you?" What I don't expect is for the most innocent question in the history of the universe to be met with:

"How's it *going*?" she says in the most withering voice imaginable. And then, just barely shy of a shout, she repeats, "How's it *going*?"

Wait. She's mad at *me*?

"You have the *nerve* to ask me that," she goes on, "after what *you've* done?"

"You're kidding me, right?"

"No."

Apparently, she has trouble grasping the concept of the rhetorical question.

"It's all your fault," she says.

"*My* fault?"

What is she even talking about?

"Dude," I say, "what are you talking about?"

"If it weren't for you and your stupid texting problem, and your stupid mother curbing your Internet access because of your stupid texting problems, my father never would have gotten the idea to do the same thing to me." Pause. "And don't call me *dude*."

"You're mad at *me*?" I don't believe this girl! "You know, if your dad"—I search for the phrase she used so I can invest it with scorn—"'curbed your Internet access,' I'm sure it's because of some idiotic thing *you* did, so you only have yourself to blame."

"Me?"

"If the shoe fits . . ."

Her lips press together so tightly, I briefly worry that her head might explode, with clouds of steam pouring out of her ears like some cartoon character.

She opens her mouth to speak but then closes it. She opens it a second time and I wait for her next explosion of infuriating anger, but instead, what comes out through gritted teeth is:

"Sorry."

"Excuse me?"

"Is there something wrong with your hearing? I said I'm sorry. Don't expect me to say it again."

I think, there's your abrupt about-face, but then wonder, what's she sorry for? But then I realize she must be sorry for how rude she was earlier.

"Oh, you're sorry for the rude way you yanked my earbuds out? Or maybe you're sorry for the ridiculous things you just said to me?" I shrug. "Don't worry. No biggie."

"No," she says, still with the gritted teeth. "I'm sorry for calling you a wimp on national television. And scared. And weak. And cowardly."

Really, she could've just stopped at *wimp*. She didn't need to go into all that detail. It's not like I'm likely to forget that whole miserable incident.

Funny thing, though, before she mentioned it, I'd gotten so caught up in . . . *interacting* with her, arguing with her about other stuff, I'd forgotten it entirely. But now her words—her *apology*—bring it all crashing back, along with my anger. I'm about to tell her what I think of her, after which of course I'll forgive her, because she did just in fact apologize, when she adds:

"My father said I had to apologize to you, that I had to be *nice* to you, and now I have." She smiles obnoxiously as she makes an all-done-with-this motion, wiping one hand against the other.

Now it's my turn to press my lips tightly together in suppressed . . . *something* . . . and grit out, "Thank you."

"You're welcome," she says perkily, her blond bun bobbing as she turns her back on me. Weird. I can't help but wonder what that hair would look like if it was let loose from its pins.

"That was—" I start to speak, but rather than finish the sentence by pointing out "sarcasm," I shake my head and then tilt it to put my earbuds back in. *Crazy loon.*

It's tilting my head that causes me to see something I hadn't noticed before. Along one wall, there's a long table with all kinds of good-looking food items on it: bagels, pastries, beverages—even the fruit looks tempting.

I have a jelly doughnut halfway to my mouth when I hear what in some cultures must be described as a panicked shriek.

"You're not going to eat *that*, are you?"

The shrieker, of course, is Katie.

"Why?" I say around a large mouthful of doughnut as she eyes the table warily like all the items on it are some kind of trap or maybe poison. "Are you worried about the camera putting ten pounds on you?" Another big bite. "Because if so, I gotta say it's too late for that." I pop the last of the doughnut into my mouth.

When I first said the word "Why?" she opened her mouth to speak, but as I kept on talking, she slowly shut it. And now that I'm completely done talking, she simply turns away and I hear a single muttered word come out of her mouth.

Wait. Did she just call me an amateur?

I'm about to express my outrage but instead I decide to just give up and listen to some music. What's the use?

The woman with the walkie-talkie comes back, warns us we've just got two minutes, and I look at Katie. For the first time, she looks nervous. And I, I don't know, feel kind of bad for her as I see her obsessively straightening her skirt. Isn't she supposed to be more experienced at these things? But then I see her putting her hand to her belly, trying to flatten something that isn't there, and it hits me:

What I said to her before—about the camera putting ten pounds on you and how it's too late to diet—perhaps she found that offensive?

Oh, man. I hate it when girls obsess about their weight. I mean, they put so much time and energy into that stuff, and for what? Sometimes, I feel like telling them, "Dudes, if you weren't spending so much time on this, you'd probably be able to take over the world!"

But there's no time to say all that, because now the woman with the walkie-talkie is warning that there's just one minute left, so there's really only time enough to say:

"You shouldn't worry about being too fat, Kat." Kat? Where did that come from? "If anything, you're too skinny."

Her expression transforms from uptight to something incalculable degrees softer and she raises her little finger toward the space between her two front teeth. When I don't immediately react, she repeats the gesture.

What? Is this sign language? Is she trying to tell me something?

I must look confused, completely lost, because she takes pity on me. Katie Willfield leans closer and, in a whisper, utters words that are kinder than anything she's ever said to me thus far:

"Dude," she says. The word sounds so awkward coming from her mouth—*dude*—and for a minute I wonder if she's mocking me. But then I realize she's just trying to speak my language as she gestures at her teeth again and adds, "You've got jelly caught between your two front teeth."

KATIE

It's not like hearing "If anything, you're too skinny" is better than being reminded that the camera puts ten pounds on you or that it's too late to diet. After all, who wants to be "too" anything? But I can tell, from the look on his face, that he means it as a kindness. As for the "too late to diet" crack, I *think* he must have meant that we are who we are and we bring that with us wherever we go—no sense in trying to change now.

Okay, maybe that's reading too much into it.

Also, did he just call me Kat?

All I know is, he does mean it kindly, which is why I felt I had to warn him about the jelly in his teeth. I can tell he's a total amateur. I continue on:

"When we're out there, don't look directly into the camera. That'll just freak the folks back home right out, like you're trying too hard. Instead, just focus on George, the interviewer. Pretend the two of you are having a private conversation and try to ignore the fact that half of America is listening in on it."

It's as I'm leaning close to him that I see that, even though he's unwedged the glob of jelly from between his teeth, he's still got white powder from the doughnut all over his face. That's going to totally show up on camera. I raise my fingers toward his face—I've never touched a boy like this before—and he just looks down at me, puzzled, but right before making contact I pull my hand back, feeling my face flush. I wonder at that flush. Is it because of embarrassment about the unprofessional nature of my behavior, almost helping out the enemy, or is at the idea of almost actually touching him?

Well, there's no need to get carried away here.

DREW

The woman with the walkie-talkie leads us out the door—past a man standing sentry who reminds me of Clint—and onto the set, which is somehow smaller than I expected it to be. There's a tall woman standing on the other side talking to some people. She has a suit on, is impossibly thin, and has a helmet of hair that looks like it wouldn't move in a force-five hurricane.

I hear a sharp intake of breath at my side as Katie mutters, "What's she doing here?"

Before I can ask who "she" is, the woman with the walkie-talkie is attaching something to the back of my shirt, shoving another something in my ear, and Helmet Hair is approaching us, hand outstretched for a shake.

"Drew, Katie," she says, "I'm Mimi Blake."

"Where's George?" Katie blurts out, shaking her hand dumbly.

"Weren't you watching the earlier segments in the green room?" the woman asks.

I shake my head. I didn't even notice the TV in the green room.

"George is on location, in Swaziland." She smiles sweetly, gesturing for us to take two seats across from her. "I'll be conducting the interview today."

The woman with the walkie-talkie says, "And we're on in 5, 4, 3 . . ."

I don't know George from Mimi, but something about Katie's reaction tells me this isn't good.

As Mimi Blake introduces us to the viewers at home, for the first time, I begin to feel nervous.

After the introductions, she continues with, "Katie, George spoke with you at length last week, so I think we'll begin today with Drew." She turns to me. "Drew. Katie has spent most of her life on the campaign trail with her father. But this is all new to you, isn't it?"

Now I officially cross over into full nervous territory as I realize that some sort of response is required from me. I stare directly into the camera. "Yes, Mimi," I say woodenly. "That is correct."

That is correct? What kind of moron talks that way?

"You're not really like any other candidate's child that we've seen in recent years."

Is there a question in there somewhere?

"Rather than dressing to impress, you dress . . ." With the back of her hand, she indicates my clothing from head to toe. Again, where's the question? And how am I supposed to respond? Too late, I remember the tie in my pocket. I can't put it on now . . . can I?

Looking directly into the camera, I say once more, "Yes, Mimi, that is correct."

I feel a sharp stabbing sensation around my ankle and realize that Katie just kicked me with the pointy toe of her green high-heeled shoe. Hey! And, ouch! Still, it does remind me of what Katie advised earlier, that I should talk directly to Mimi, not the camera, like we're just two people having a conversation.

This immediately reduces my level of nervousness. And you know what else reduces it? Anger at Katie for getting me into this mess in the first place.

As anger fuels me from the inside, on the outside I suddenly feel distinctly calmer. And, as Mimi proceeds to ask me questions, I realize that this is easy. I know these questions! And how do I know them? Because the TV network forwarded them to Ann in advance to show to me. And *that* happened, according to Ann, because Katie's people set a precedent last time by insisting that that was the only way Katie would do the interview with them—if she could see the questions first. This struck me as cheating at the time. What kind of *wimp* needs to know the questions in advance? What could she possibly be scared of? Coward. But her fear is serving me well now as Mimi continues, "We're told that, despite your family's relatively recent elevation in fortune—unlike the Willfields, the Reillys weren't born with silver spoons in their mouths—you still ride the public school bus and even go to your old public school. Is that correct?"

"Yeah, Mimi." Look at me! No more robotic "Yes, Mimi, that is correct" for me. I'm nailing this thing! "I'm a big believer in public transportation," I add. "I even took the train here today."

"Well, don't think you'll be able to do that once you're in the White House," Katie blurts out, adding a muttered, "not that that'll ever happen."

What is it with that girl? And why does she get under my skin so much?

Oh, right. She's annoying.

Plus, could she be right? If my mom wins, will my life really be that different? Excuse me while I retreat back into denial.

I decide to ignore Katie. Mimi does too, practically cooing at me, "Ooh, a real man of the people!"

She swivels her head sharply from me to Katie. I take this to mean that the camera will be swiveling to Katie now too, so I take this opportunity to whip my tie from my pocket and rapidly knot it around my neck. The ends wind up wildly uneven, but whatever.

After a dramatic pause and with a fake smile, Mimi says in a falsely cheerful tone that couldn't be more menacing: "*Katie*."

Just her name, full stop.

I have no idea exactly what's coming next. What I do know is that for Katie, it can't be good.

But for me? This is going to be very good. Because there's nothing I can imagine enjoying more than seeing my enemy fall on her face.

KATIE

After Mimi's menacing "*Katie*," she turns to the camera and says, "We'll hear from Katie Willfield after the break," and we pause briefly for commercials.

I can't say for certain what Mimi has in store for me once the break's over. All I know is, it'll be harder than those puffball questions she's been lobbing at Drew. Why, she's all but asking him, with moony eyes, to tell us all the reasons he's so wonderful.

Ugh.

She'll undoubtedly ask me some of the harder questions that George left on the table. Like if I ever felt shortchanged, growing up in a single-parent household in which the only parent spent most of his time focusing on his political career? Or if I have political ambitions of my own?

Both of those would be harder than the questions asked on the previous visit because they're more personal. But that's okay. I'm a professional. And I know how to use the personal professionally. The first question, I'll answer by saying, I don't feel shortchanged at all. When a candidate is as fit to lead the country as my father is, I can only feel privileged, *blessed* to be a part of his manifest destiny. And if it's the second? I'll say, It's a little premature to throw my hat into the ring, don't you think? and I'll accompany it with a smile and a wink to let everyone know that, of *course* that's in my future!

Oh, no. But what if, worst of all, she asks about the china patterns? There was nothing on the list of original questions about that but since George put it on the table with his comments, maybe it is considered fair game now? Still not a problem, I think as I stiffen my back. I'll just fall on my sword. I'll say, My father had no knowledge of what I was doing. Voters should not penalize themselves over childish high jinks that are my sole responsibility. And if she follows it up by questioning, Shouldn't a parent know what his child is up to? Well, she won't do that, because she'll know that I could then counter with a question about her own lax parenting style, and believe me, she *won't* want to go there. Everyone knows the Blake kids are nothing but tabloid trouble.

As we're counted back down from commercial break and Mimi opens again with that eerie smile, followed by "*Katie*," I'm feeling *pret*-ty good about my various strategies.

Then Mimi says, "Is it true what we've heard, that even though you're sixteen, you've *never* had a romantic relationship in your life?"

What? She can't ask that!

"Is it true you've never even been on a single date?"

I'm being blindsided here! How is it possible that she can do this? We had an agreement! These questions weren't on the list! But then, with horror, it hits me: That agreement was for my *last* appearance on the show. We never had them sign one for *this* appearance.

Mimi leans forward in her chair and I can practically *feel* the camera moving in for a close-up of my humiliation.

"Is it true, Katie, that you've never been kissed?"

DREW

So for me? Actually? Seeing my enemy, my nemesis, fall on her face?

Not good. Not so good at all. Three short questions may not seem like much of a barrage, but that's what it undoubtedly becomes as Mimi keeps hitting into Katie with rude question after rude question. A part of me thinks I should be enjoying this—I *want* to be enjoying this. After what Katie's done to me, she deserves whatever she gets. But the thing is, she doesn't. No one does.

While I'm thinking this, *another* part of me recognizes a shocking truth: Katie's not just cute. She's beautiful. The line of questioning and her obvious discomfort have brought out more color in her cheeks and made her green eyes sparkle. As she shifts in her chair, I notice the skirt of her crazy power suit is tight enough to show off what is undeniably an excellent pair of legs. *Wow*.

I see Katie open her mouth but no words come out. She opens it again and it occurs to me, even if she does manage to speak, she's obviously so hurt, so crumpled by this, I doubt she'll be able to help her own cause.

"Buses!" I suddenly shout.

Mimi whips her head at me. "Ex*cuse* me?"

"Buses! And trains! And . . . and . . . and subways! Did I forget before to mention subways? Really, any and all forms of public transportation—I can't say enough good things about it. I just love the stuff."

"That's terrific, Drew. Like I said, a real man of the people. But we were focusing on—"

"And the most ultimate form of public transportation of all . . ." Did I really just say "most ultimate"? My English teacher would kill me. "Your feet!" I hold up my own two, clad in boots, to illustrate. For good measure, I waggle them around for a bit.

"Whoever invented feet," I add, "they did one heckuva job."

No matter how many times Mimi tries to yank the interview back to Katie, I just yank it right back with more of what will undoubtedly go down in television history as "The Ode to Public Transportation."

As Mimi, with no other choice, finally wraps things up, I thrust my hand out for a shake. "Thank you, Mimi." I shake extra firmly. "And I hope I've made myself clear here today: I just *love* public transportation!"

Two minutes later, we're collecting our personal items from the green room—her purse, my iPod and Game Boy—and two minutes after that, we're waiting for the elevator, the Clint-like guy behind us. Despite all the people bustling past, it's like there's a cone of silence surrounding us. Wow, is this awkward.

I want to ask her if she's okay after what Mimi pulled. I want to say *something* to show support for what she just went through. But I can't find the words. Won't whatever I say just draw more attention to what happened? Make it worse? If only I could find the right words to—

At last, the elevator arrives. Katie steps on first, followed by doppelgänger Clint, and looks back out at me.

"You know," she says, "there was no need for you to interfere like that. I could have handled that all by myself. I've certainly dealt with worse than the likes of Mimi Blake in my life."

Then she punches a button.

As the elevator door starts to close, I yell through the ever-decreasing gap, "Yeah, well, *thank you* works too!"

KATIE

I exit the special door on the side of the studio, only to find the usual gaggle of stage-door Johnnys and Janes waiting there. It's a strangely larger gaggle than usual, mostly female, and mostly fairly young. As they call out things to me—"Is it true you've never been on a date, Katie? Is it true you've never been kissed?"—I wonder bitterly: Shouldn't a lot of these people be at school by now?

Their questions make me realize that they must have watched the interview on the jumbo TV the studio keeps outside for the crowds that gather every morning. All I can do is stride proudly through the gaggle, hold my head up high, and keep the burn out of my face and a smile plastered on. Their taunting questions follow me to the limo, where Kent immediately opens the door. It's all I can do to keep reminding myself of my mantra: eye on the prize!

But after I slide into the back of the limo, and Kent gently shuts the door, I allow my face to fall into my hands. I know I'm protected from prying eyes by the tinted glass. *Oh, the embarrassment. Oh, the humiliation.*

"Are you okay, Miss Katie?" Kent asks, settling into the front seat.

I don't answer right away. I don't answer because I don't think I can, not without crying. With the amount of time we've spent together over the past few weeks, Kent is starting to feel as close of a friend as Dog. His being worried about me only makes the impulse to cry worse. Originally, I'd planned on going straight from the studio to Willfield Academy, just like I did for my triumphant return after my interview last week. I smile ruefully as I remember that that wasn't exactly triumphant either. But after this? I can't show my face there today. I'm not sure I'll ever be able to again.

"Miss Katie?" Kent tries again.

I'm about to instruct him to just drive, to just take me home so I can hide away forever—or at least until it's time to move into the White House—when I hear something.

Even though the morning is brisk, Kent has opened the very tops of the windows to get some fresh air. That sound I'm hearing now? It's the gaggle, growing louder. I look up and out the window. I'm not sure what I'm expecting. Maybe for the gaggle to attack me and demand I answer their questions as though I'm a dictator in a banana republic? (Not the store.) What I see instead is Drew Reilly.

He's being absolutely mobbed by the young female members of the gaggle. Not only are they yelling questions at him, they're actually *touching* him.

What's the matter with him? Doesn't he know to just stride right on through as quickly as possible? And now they're chanting his name, like he's one of those rock stars. Oh, great. I get scorn. And what does he get? Adulation.

Disgusted, now I'm *really* ready to tell Kent to just drive on—nothing to see here!—only I see two teenage girls, each holding on to the ends of Drew's tie. When did he find time to put that on? Did I miss something? And just look at that knot. He really needs someone to teach him how to properly tie a full Windsor. As the two girls each pull a different end of the tie and a third girl yanks the beanie off Drew's head and races off down the street, it occurs to me that they're trying for souvenirs! The only problem is, the two fighting over the tie are neglecting the small fact that Drew's neck is still in the middle.

Watching him claw at the tightening tie with his fingers, I climb back out of the limo. "Amateurs," I grumble to myself, thinking that Drew would never be in this current mess if he knew what he was doing. I stride up to Drew and his hangers-on. "Let him go," I command one teenage girl. "Unhand him," I snap at the other. Am I being too formal here? Perhaps. But in my experience, an imperious tone can do wonders. Sure enough, startled, they obey. Before they get a chance to realize that it's two against one and lurch for the tie again, I grab Drew by the shirt and tug him quickly toward the open back door of the limo. Once there, I let go of his shirt and shove him inside, hearing the clicks of cameras going off all the while. *Oh, no*, I groan inwardly as I climb in after him, *no doubt this'll be all over TMZ by the time we hit Connecticut.* Because while the mainstream media may stick to the Clinton precedent of laying off the minor children of presidential candidates, there's no similar understanding from the lesser mainstream media or any jerk with a cell phone. And while I would love media attention, I don't want or need any more that's related to Drew Reilly.

Oh, well. I'll just do damage control later. I'm good at that.

"Drive, Kent," I say firmly.

Like the professional Kent is, he zooms away from the curb, no questions asked.

"You know," I point out to Drew, "that back there wouldn't have happened to you if you brought a Secret Service agent like Kent with you, Mr. I Took the Train in Today."

Beside me, Drew is out of breath. I've never been physically mobbed by a gaggle of girls before, but I'm guessing that'll do that to a guy. When Drew does finally speak, he sounds angry. And, I soon realize, he's angry at me.

"You know," he says, "you didn't have to do anything. I could have totally handled the situation all by myself."

"Seriously?" I've never actually said that like it's a sarcastic interrogative before—but I've certainly seen enough kids do it on TV, and, I must say, it feels good. "Yeah, well," I add, *thank you* works too."

Drew just glares at me.

I glare right back.

And then we both burst out laughing.

We laugh hysterically, like nothing funnier has ever happened in the world. I've never laughed like this with someone my age before. It feels so good. We laugh until there's nothing left in us and we trail off, almost forgetting what set us off in the first place.

"Gosh, I'm hungry," I say.

Drew snorts. "You should have had something back at the green room."

I wave a dismissive hand. "That's for amateurs."

"What do you mean?" he asks.

I explain the perils of getting food on your face or stuck between your teeth, finishing with, "Like you did, with the jelly from that doughnut. And—" I start to add but then stop myself.

But that Drew, he's a quick one.

"And?" he prompts.

"Nothing."

"*And?*" he prompts more forcefully, leaving me no choice.

"I have a confession to make."

"Still waiting here."

"You didn't just get jelly between your teeth."

"No?"

"You also got white powdered sugar all over your face."

"All over it?"

"Well, just one side."

"And you let me go on camera like that, on national TV?"

"Like I said, it's just one side."

"You should've said something."

"And I almost did!" I say in my own defense. "But I'd already told you about the jelly and I figured, no need to get carried away."

He looks at me, his eyes stormy—I never noticed how brown his eyes were before, how gentle and warm—and I think: Oh, no. Here it comes. We had one good moment together and now he's mad and I've just gone and spoiled everything.

But instead of yelling at me like I expect him to, Drew bursts out laughing again.

"You're not mad?" I say incredulously.

"Maybe for a second," he says. "But you know, you got me—so, good one! I mean, powdered sugar—how mad can I be?" He laughs again. Then: "But wait, how foolish did I look out there?"

I hold my forefinger and thumb about an eighth of an inch apart.

"Is it still there?" He rubs his palm against his jaw.

"Yes," I say, "but higher." I raise my hand to his face, like I did what now seems like a lifetime ago, only this time I make contact. His skin is warm beneath my touch, rougher than my own, masculine. Hand trembling slightly, I gently brush the remaining powdered sugar away. "All gone now," I say, slightly sorry for not having an excuse to leave my fingers there. "Like it never happened."

When he doesn't say anything back, I fill the silence with, "I suppose you need to get back to school."

"Nah, I'm taking the rest of the day off. You?"

"Day off." Pause. "I'm still hungry." Pause. "You?"

Drew shrugs. "I could eat."

DREW

The last time anyone wiped sugar from my face it was my mom, when I was little. That act and the accompanying touch made me feel taken care of, secure. But when Katie touched me, it made me feel the opposite of secure. Truth? It was more like that moment at the top of a roller coaster, right before the drop, when your stomach clenches and you're simultaneously terrified yet aching to tip over the edge.

And, of course, I didn't want the moment to end.

Incredibly flaky layers of pastry with cream in between. Pink glaze. Purple sugar crystals on top. I've never been a big pink-and-purple foods kind of guy, but *man*.

"So this is what a Cronut's like," I say appreciatively as I take another large bite.

"So this is what playing hooky is like," Katie says, as she takes another bite of her own Cronut.

"Wait." I swallow. "You've never played hooky before?"

"You have?"

"Well, sure."

"And you don't get in trouble for it?"

"I do, but I kind of figure I'm doing my teachers a favor."

"How so?"

I shrug. "How can people miss me if I never go away?"

Katie looks at me for a moment, dead serious, and then she busts out laughing.

Before today, with what little I'd seen of her on TV and in the newspapers, I never would have pictured that she could laugh like this. But when she does, it's like all the buttoned-up . . . *Katieness* in her falls away, and what's left is . . .

I'm not sure I have words for it. But it's like, for the first time, she seems like a real person, maybe even a person I'd want to get to know better.

Well, I shouldn't get carried away.

Still . . .

"You think this is hooky?" I indicate the safety of the limo around us with my Cronut-holding hand.

"You mean it's not?"

"Well, no. For this to be any good, we'd need to go somewhere or do something."

"Like where? Or what? When you play hooky—you know, to do your teachers a *favor*—where do you like to go?"

I tell her.

"Kent!" Katie calls up front to her Secret Service agent. She tells him where we want to go.

"Are you sure about this?" I say.

"Why wouldn't I be?"

"Well, like, don't you have to get home or something?"

"My father's in Kansas, campaigning. He'll be on the road mostly for the next seven weeks, campaigning straight through until Election Day. You?"

"My mom left right after breakfast this morning for South Carolina. Or was it Virginia?"

"She does need to worry about the South," Katie muses.

I keep forgetting that she knows a lot more about this stuff than I do.

"Kent, did you hear me?" she calls.

"I don't know about this, Miss Katie," Kent says.

"Kent?"

"What would your father—"

"Kent."

"Yes, Miss Katie."

I'm not sure I entirely approve of the way she takes charge of the assigned help, but I must admit, the girl does know how to get things done.

For the remainder of the ride, we mostly talk about the one thing we know we share in common, the one thing we both like.

"I can't believe how good these Cronuts are," I say, taking a second from the box between us.

"I can't believe you never had one before today," she says, taking another one for herself.

But a few minutes later, when she reaches for a third, I pass.

"I thought you were on a diet," I say.

"Do I look like I'm on a diet?" She takes a healthy bite. "Why would you say that?"

"Back in the green room, you practically shrieked at me when I took that doughnut."

"I did not *practically shriek*. And anyway, I thought you understood by now that only amateurs eat in the green room."

"Right." I feel myself tightening up. For a moment there, I had forgotten who I'm dealing with. "Amateurs."

"Well, it's true." She shrugs. "But once the show is over . . ." She happily takes another bite.

I have to admit, I've never seen a girl eat like this before. And, no sooner do I think this than I blurt it out.

"I've never seen a girl eat like you before."

"Why? Am I messy?" She puts a hand to her cheek and rubs. There is some frosting on her face but it's on the other side and I don't say anything about it.

"It's not that. It's just all the girls at school . . ."

"What about them?"

"They're always on diets."

"All of them?"

"Pretty much. I mean, at least, that's what I think they want everyone to think."

"I'm not sure I'm following."

"Take lunch, for example. No matter their individual size, they all eat salads and diet soda. Sometimes I think they think that if no one actually sees them eating real food, then people will think—well, I'm not even sure what they're hoping people will think. Maybe that they always eat like that, even when no one's looking? That they can't really be whatever size they are because clearly they don't eat enough?"

"Salads are real food," she counters.

"Not like Cronuts," I counter right back.

"True," she concedes, closing her eyes in bliss as she takes another bite.

"Do you eat like this all the time?" I ask.

"I thought you said I was too skinny."

Back at the green room, I did say that. And now, I don't even know why. Because the truth is, she's not *too* anything, at least not when it comes to size. She just looks . . . healthy.

"You don't have one of those eating disorders, do you? Like, you eat all this stuff and then get rid of it somehow?"

She laughs. "I don't have time for anything like that."

"Then how is it that you're not fat?"

"I guess I'm always just so busy running around doing stuff. Plus, I just eat when I'm hungry." She shrugs, stares at the remainder of her third Cronut, and clearly considers eating it before tossing the last bite back into the box and closing the lid. "And I stop eating before I'm full."

Wow, what a concept.

• • •

"Wow! So, this is where you go to play hooky!" Katie says, tripping her way through the sand, Kent following at a discreet distance. "Where is everybody, though?"

"School's in session," I point out, "plus, it's a weekday. You might see joggers first thing in the morning, or the occasional person walking a dog. But other than that? Not many people come out."

As if to prove my point, one lone person jogs past us toward the water with a dog on a leash.

"Wow!" she says again, taking in the sand all around us, the sky overhead, the water straight in front. "So, this is the beach!"

We're at the one I've been going to since I was little, the closest one to the old neighborhood.

"Come on." I laugh. "Don't tell me you've never been to the beach!"

"Of course I have," she says stiffly. Then: "Well, when I was young, and we'd take vacations, sometimes we'd go."

"Never since then? But you live in Connecticut. There are lots of beaches."

"We have a pool."

"You live in Willfield, for crying out loud, which is supposed to have the best beach in the state!"

"You know where I live?"

If she was Sandy, I'd chuck something at her for saying something so stupid. "Come on, Alien from Another Planet, let me introduce you to the beach. Kat, this is the beach." I wave my arm out. "Beach, meet Kat."

She blushes and I'm not sure what at. Am I embarrassing her somehow?

But as she stumbles along at my side, I can't help but point out, "You know, it'd be easier to walk in the sand if you take your shoes off."

"You still have yours on."

"They're boots," I say, "and they're not high heels."

She bends over to remove her green high heels, but teeters on the uneven surface, overbalancing herself. Without thinking about it, I reach out a hand and grab her firmly by the elbow to steady her so she doesn't fall. It's funny. I instinctively do it, out of politeness. But no sooner does my hand grasp her elbow than I feel a peculiar *rightness*, not to mention a physical charge that's kind of unsettling.

She flinches at my touch. I don't understand. Is she worried I'm going to hurt her?

"Sorry." She blushes again, dropping her gaze. "I'm not accustomed to people I know touching me."

Not acc—

What does she mean? No high fives from people in her classes, ever? No hugs from her girlfriends at school? (I know girls do this because I've seen them, many times. And all too often, these hugs are accompanied by high-pitched squeals that I've often thought were designed to puncture human eardrums.)

What kind of strange life has this girl lived?

"That's better," she says, her feet finally free. She squishes her toes in the sand, clearly enjoying the sensation on her skin. "So," she says more brightly, "what is it that you do when you're playing hooky at the beach?"

I gesture with my chin toward the lifeguard tower. "I sit up there."

"Okay, then!" she says in this overly gung-ho voice, like she's game to do whatever the natives do.

When we're at the base of the tower, I figure she might need my help getting up, and I hold out my hand. After all, with that green suit on with its pencil skirt snug around her upper thighs, I figure it might be too constricting for her to climb up without assistance. But she ignores my hand, shimmying right past me like a suited nanny goat, and all I can do is shimmy up next to her. When I get to the top, she's already sitting but moves over so I can plop down beside her on the wide wooden bench seat.

She swings her legs for a few minutes, staring out at the view. Then: "Well, this is nice!"

A few minutes more of silent leg swinging passes, followed by: "So what else do you do when you come here?"

"Look at the view." I shrug. "Think about stuff. Solve the problems of the world."

"Oh." Then: "Okay, then!"

The problem is that it's impossible to think about the things I normally do with her here. Particularly when her suit skirt is once again riding up and showing off her legs. If anyone had asked me before today if I was a woman's-suit guy, I'd have said no way! That was always Sandy's peculiar thing. I would have said I preferred short shorts and bikinis, in no particular order. But this buttoned-up exterior coupled with a flash of leg—and oh, those legs!—now, I can definitely see the appeal.

Focus, Drew. Resist the optical allure of those legs. I think about the questions that awful Mimi Blake person asked her back at the TV station. Has Katie really never had a romance? Never been on a date? Never been kissed?

I mean, I'm no Casanova, but we're both sixteen—well, just barely. I've had my fair share of experiences. Haven't most kids had at least . . . *something* by now?

I have a powerful urge to ask about Mimi Blake's questions but of course I don't because, one, it would be too awkward, and two, it hits me that Katie's reaction is my answer. She wasn't just blindsided by questions she hadn't been told were coming. She was embarrassed at the truth. Still, maybe I'm wrong.

So, I try to beat around the bush with:

"You must have a lot of friends—you know, at your school?"

"Oh, no!" She laughs. "I don't have time for all that!"

"What do you mean? How can you not have time to have friends?"

"I'm always too busy helping my father campaign!" she says as though the answer must be obvious. Then: "Oh, that's right. You're relatively new to all this. Well, you'll learn."

No, I won't, I think. I don't want to learn how to not have a life.

"But what do you do when you're not busy campaigning?"

"Do?" She looks mildly perplexed. "I blog." And now she looks peeved. "Well, I used to, before you lost your tech privileges for doing something stupid and then my father heard about it and then, after I made one *teeny-tiny* blog post about china patterns, decided that your mother's no-tech policy was the way to—"

"Yeah, I think we adequately covered that one already. I'm good, thanks."

"And I hang out with Dog."

"Dog?"

"My cat."

"Of course."

A cat named Dog? This girl is just so kooky. But adorable too. And funny. I wonder if she realizes how funny she is.

"Well, how about you?" she asks defiantly. "What do you do for fun and excitement?"

She says those last three words with what I think must be the most derision with which they've ever been said. Still, pushing aside my initial annoyance, I find myself telling her about Sandy.

As I speak about our friendship, now stretching back well over a decade, a look comes over her face, like I'm telling her about some strange state or country she's heard about, but never traveled to herself. Like Idaho or Uruguay.

Well, she's probably been to Idaho. You know, on the campaign trail.

For someone so self-absorbed, she's a surprisingly good listener. So I find myself discussing the other thing I do with my free time, restoring the vintage Corvair I bought.

"And what will you do with it once it's fully restored?" she asks.

"By then I should have my license. I'll drive it, of course."

She laughs.

"What's so funny?"

"You think you'll ever get to actually *drive* that car?"

And now she's laughing harder than she has since we shared that first big laugh back in the limo.

"Why wouldn't I? I'm sixteen and two months. Connecticut state law dictates that a person can get a restricted license at sixteen and four months. Did I mention it's the law? Look it up."

"Yes, I know," she says. "I also read an article in the *Times* recently that said kids are getting their licenses later and later these days. They spend so much time texting each other, they feel as though they're doing social things together even though they really don't go out. So they don't feel as much need to get a license to drive places like previous generations did."

"Well, that's not me."

"Anyway, that wasn't what I was laughing at."

"What, then?"

"I was laughing because if your mother wins the election, your life won't be your own!"

"It won't?"

"Of course not! You'll have Secret Service people trailing you twenty-four seven!"

"I don't want that!"

"Well, you won't be able to do anything about that. Come to think of it, why *don't* you have an agent assigned to you?"

"Because I declined. When someone's still just a nominee, or a member of the family of a nominee, you can decline. So while the rest of my family got them, I declined. Have some guy in a suit and dark glasses, trailing me everywhere I go? In *gym class*? No, thank you."

"Really? Because I wish Kent would go to gym class with me."

"And that's where we differ." *One of the million ways,* I think.

"But like I said, if your mom is elected . . ." She pauses. "I can't believe you thought if your mom was elected that somehow your life could go on the same as always."

Because I'm in denial? Heavy-duty, head-in-the-sand denial? Or maybe because I've secretly thought that my mom could never win, so I'd never really have to face that day?

But I can't say that to her. I still have trouble just saying all that to myself.

"Of course," she says, "that will never happen. Your having to deal with the Secret Service."

"It won't?" Maybe there's a loophole?

"Of *course* not. Your mom will *never* beat my father."

The funny thing is that I don't even want my mom to win the election—especially not now that Katie has forced me to admit to myself what my life will be like if she does. Obviously a part of me has never really believed that my mom *can* win the election. But Katie saying that? So scornfully? Suddenly, a small part of me wants my mom to win.

No matter how much I've enjoyed spending time with Katie today, in the end, she's still the enemy.

"Ah," I say, "I think that's just about enough hooky for one day."

The limo pulls up in front of my house, neither of us speaking the whole ride back.

"Wow," Katie says, looking out the window, "you live pretty nicely for a Democrat."

What do you even say to something like that?

"Thank you for the ride, Kent," I say, climbing out.

I'm about to just slam the door when I hear Katie's voice.

"Thank you for a lovely afternoon, Drew," she says, hand thrust straight out for a shake. "It was fun finally learning how to play hooky."

There's the thing about Katie: She can be so maddeningly infuriating—with her self-absorption and her insensitivity and all her "We are *so* going to beat you!"—and in the next second she'll do something that will show me just how small her life has been, just how vulnerable she is. Somehow, it moves me.

I bypass her outstretched hand and touch my fingers to her cheek. She only flinches for a second and then relaxes against my hand. It feels so, so soft, and her eyes look so, so green.

"What are you doing?" she asks.

Something I've wanted to do for hours, I think. But what I say is, "You had some Cronut on your cheek." She blushes.

"Good luck with your car and your life and the election." She pauses. "Well, maybe not the last part."

"Yeah, same to you."

And then I'm gone.

KATIE

Well, that was nice.

Wait. Did that qualify as a date?

Hmm . . . probably not.

Still, once inside the house I lean my back against the closed door and sigh, remembering the feel of his fingers lingering against my cheek. I'm pretty sure I didn't have any Cronut there. *Maybe*, I think hopefully, Drew just wanted to touch me? Is that even possible?

And was it in my head, or did I occasionally catch him trying to steal glances at me? It probably was in my head and yet now that I'm alone, I'm forced to admit: I was definitely stealing glances at him. Up close, he was so shockingly cute; startlingly handsome, even.

I sigh again and then head straight for the kitchen, hoping for a snack, only to find Cook there.

Cook, for the record, does have a real name and I even know what it is. But Cook is also a huge fan of *General Hospital* and apparently the Quartermaines—the wealthy family on that soap opera—always refer to their chef like that. Cook, in turn, insists we do the same. She says that somehow it makes her feel more elegant. I'm not sure I entirely get this, but it makes her happy.

"How are the poll numbers today, Cook?" I ask now.

Cook has always been very protective of Daddy's numbers.

"About the same. The senator is leading that woman by three percentage points but there is still seven percent for 'Don't Know.' Those Don't Knows always bother me. What is *wrong* with people in this country? Are they just not paying attention? With only seven weeks to go, how can they still not know?"

"Don't worry, Cook. If we just get three-sevenths of the Don't Know seven percent, we still win." I reach for the handle on the fridge.

"Don't touch that door!" Cook warns. "I'm making chicken-fried steak and biscuits with gravy for your dinner tonight in the hopes of working some magic with the senator's numbers in the South. I don't want you to spoil your appetite."

Almost nothing ever spoils my appetite. Still.

"Okay," I say, stepping away from the fridge, since twelve years of her cooking for us has taught me that there's no arguing with Cook.

"The *big* problem," Cook says, rolling out some dough for the biscuits, "is that man down in Georgia."

I know who she's talking about. If Drew's mom is always "that woman" to Cook, then "that man down in Georgia" can only be Bix Treadwell, billionaire, the third-party Independent candidate.

"What's Bix done now?" I ask.

"Rising in the polls, that's what he's done!"

"How is that possible? You just said my father and Drew's—" I catch myself and continue—"and that woman are still neck and neck, with Daddy ahead by three percent."

"And they are! But they've each *dropped* by two percent!"

"Bix Treadwell has gained four percent since the last poll? How'd he manage to do that?"

"Only three percent. Don't Know increased by one percent. And he's probably managed to do it by making people all kinds of crazy promises you know he can't keep. Free cable TV and a chicken in every pot, my foot."

"Aw, don't worry about it, Cook." I put my arm around her and give her shoulders a big squeeze. "Third-party candidates never go anywhere."

"Well, they could. Just because a thing has never happened doesn't mean it won't."

"True. And it might still happen someday, but not until after we're all long gone." I give her another squeeze. I'm not really the hugging type, but it's my experience that when Cook gets too worked up about one of Daddy's campaigns, the cooking tends to suffer.

"I just hope you're right," she says, wiping her hands on her apron. "Oh, I almost forgot—your dad called for you!"

"He did?" I'm about to add, Why didn't you tell me right away? and How could you forget that? but I know it's easier for Cook to forget things these days. She's getting old.

"Yes, about at least a dozen times. He said to call him as soon as you get in. Since you're not allowed to use your cell phone anymore, here."

She hands me her iPhone. On the list of galling things in my life, it ranks high that Cook has 24/7 access to state-of-the-art technology while I do not.

"Thanks," I say, already hitting my father's number. What could he possibly need so badly that he called a dozen times?

Wait. Could this mean he's finally firing droopy-mustached Marvin and hiring me full-time as his campaign manager?

My heart's so busy pounding with anticipation that as I wait for my father to pick up—*pick up, Pick Up, PICK UP!*—I barely register Dog, up from his nap, snaking around my ankles in hopes of a treat.

"Pumpkin!"

"Daddy, what's wrong? Is everything okay on the campaign trail?"

"Everything's fine. Fine! Of course, by the third diner stop, I did start feeling full, but you know you can't do those appearances without eating—people think you're snobby if you don't accept their culinary hospitality and then you lose their votes. And, sadly, I'm pretty sure that last baby I kissed had a cold."

"Be sure to take extra vitamin C, Daddy, and you'll be fine. The campaign trail is no place for a runny nose."

"Right. We don't want a repeat of what happened last spring." He laughs.

"It's no laughing matter! Remember, just because you had the flu, your Republican opponents in the primary started those rumors about you being a cokehead? We definitely do not want to go through all that again. A drippy nose is your worst enemy."

"That's my girl, always looking out for my best interests."

The way he says that, the pride in his voice . . .

Is this my big moment, finally? I'm ready to scream, Good-bye, Willfield Academy! And hello, bad diner food and kissing sniveling babies! But I don't want to be too obvious. There's no point in putting the cart before the horse unless you're prepared to . . .

Ah, I don't even know how to end that. I just know I shouldn't overplay my hand.

"I'm sure you didn't call a dozen times," I say, "just to talk over old cokehead accusations."

"Of course not."

Inside, I'm squealing: *SQUEE! Here it comes—here it comes!*

"I called to talk to you about your performance on *That Morning Show.*"

What? I stare at the phone. What?

After recovering from my shock as well as I can, I put the phone back to my head and hear:

"—that I said to be nice—"

"Hold on a second, Daddy. Could you back this train up and start again?"

"What's wrong with you today, pumpkin? You don't seem yourself. I said I know I told you to be nice to that Reilly boy, but don't you think you took things a bit too far?"

There's a pit in my stomach. "What do you mean?"

"You protected him from that mob of girls after the show!"

Oh, no. "How did you know about that? I thought you were eating in diners and kissing sick babies all day."

"Know about it? Everybody knows about it—it's all over the YouTube!"

How did I forget about the lesser mainstream media and the people outside of the studios? Darn camera phones. I think I know why I forgot briefly: because I was actually enjoying being with Drew. I was so caught up in the moment, I took my eye off the prize.

The pit in my stomach grows, but I can't help myself from correcting, "It's not *the* YouTube, Daddy, it's just YouTube. And while we're at it, it's not the Facebook either. Or the Twitter or—"

"I don't need a social-media coach at the moment, thank you very much, sweetie pie."

All these "pumpkins" and "sweetie pies"—I think my father has definitely been spending too much time campaigning in the South. At the rate he's going, by the time we're in the White House, he'll be calling me his "baby grits" or something.

Before I can respond, he continues, "And then Kent informs me that you gave that boy *Cronuts* and you took him to the *beach*?"

Darn that Kent. What a rat fink.

"What were you thinking, Katie?"

At least this time he didn't call me dumpling or something.

What was I thinking of? I was thinking that I felt bad for Drew. The poor guy was about to get his head decapitated by those two girls using his scarf like a wishbone at Thanksgiving dinner. Then, later? I thought it would be fun to play hooky like a normal kid. And at the beach, I thought how *nice* it felt to actually spend time with a kid my own age—a boy even!— for a change. Of course I knew it wasn't a *date*—not like I almost went on with Jayson. Okay, I know that wasn't any-thing—but it was at least something. Someday, I might even have a real friend.

But I can't tell any of that to Daddy right now—he'd never understand me feeling anything positive having to do with the enemy. Thankfully it looks like I don't have to, because Daddy suddenly crows: "I know why you did it!"

"You do?"

"Of course! And I must say, apple pie, you are brilliant— brilliant!"

"I am? I mean, I am."

"Of course! Why, you're just lulling the opposition into a false sense of security, making the boy think you're friends. Then, when he lets his guard down, you'll absorb whatever intel you can get out of him and bring it back to me. I must say, it's a touch Machiavellian, even for you—but I have to admit, even Marvin couldn't come up with a better plan."

"Yeah," I say, stunned dumb, "that's me, a real Machiavel-lian."

I'm so stunned by this dark view of what I thought of as such a light, fun, *nice* afternoon, I barely register the stuff he says next, the apologies about Mimi Blake blindsiding me with personal questions along with a vow to "send the network a sternly worded letter!"

And when my father says to "keep up the good work," it's all I can do to ignore the now gaping hole in my stomach as I quietly reply, "I'll try, Daddy."

DREW

As I turn the key in the lock, I can't help but think about the sensation of Katie's face against my fingers—how is it possible for someone who exudes such a tough exterior to feel so soft? And on top of that: *Why is it I can't stop thinking about her?* I walk through the door, only to find Sandy sitting halfway up the sweeping staircase in the central entry hall.

"How'd you get here? Who let you in?" I ask.

"I took the bus," he says. "'The nanny'"—he pauses to curl his fingers in air quotes—"let me in."

Normally I am opposed to air quotes just on general principle, but in this instance they're fully justified. "The nanny" is Stella, the woman my mom hired a while back when she became busy with the campaign. Also because, even though my dad hardly ever goes out on the road with her, for some reason he's almost never home anymore. I guess that even though he made his big invention years ago and got the big paycheck for it, he's still out working on stuff. Or maybe he's taken up golf? Anyway, the nanny is here to keep an eye on the twins when he's not around. The nanny is also here to keep an eye on me, I suppose.

"Dude," Sandy says, "what did you do today?"

I don't know what he's talking about, but there's an uneasy feeling in my stomach as I ask, "What do you mean?"

Instead of answering he says, "So tell me, was she hot? Because you know what I think about females in suits, that underneath all that buttoned-up properness, they're all—"

"What do you mean?" I cut him off.

"Dude, it's all over YouTube and TMZ." He holds up his iPhone.

Just because I can't use mine there's no rule stating I can't use his, so I grab it from him, look at the screen.

The first thing I see is the picture: it's of me, my neck being strangled by my own tie. My mouth is yawning wide like that guy in the famous painting, *The Scream*, and one eye is popping while the other is shut tight. If I didn't know the guy in the picture, I'd think: what a dork.

I scroll down and see the next picture, a startled-looking me being tugged along by Katie.

And the last picture: Katie shoving me into the limo.

"Look at the headline," Sandy prompts.

I scroll back up and there I see it, in screaming print:

CELEBRICAL SOULMATES???

"Celebrical?" I blink. "What's that?"

"A mash-up of celebrity and political. I'm thinking they didn't go with the reverse because, who'd ever be able to figure out how to pronounce politicity?"

Oh, no. I start to read the accompanying article:

They say that politics makes strange bedfellows. Well, in this instance, those bedfellows are teens . . .

What?! I can't read this nonsense!

And yet somehow I do: three long paragraphs about me and Katie, one about her, one about me, and the last one about us together—*as a couple*—detailing how we have the potential to be the hottest couple since that boy-band pop star and one of those chicks who practically grew up on the Disney Channel.

When I'm done I dumbly hand the phone back to Sandy.

"So," he says again, all eager, "was she hot?"

"It wasn't like that!"

No sooner are the words out of my mouth than I realize I'd have been better off playing it cool, laughing it off, because what Sandy comes back at me with is: "Oh my God, you like her!"

"No, I *don't!*"

Wait, a part of me wonders. Do I? I mean, I do think she's cute and all. Not just cute—she's beautiful.

"But you do. It's like you're standing up for her honor or something."

"No, I'm not! I'm just saying . . ."

"Saying what?"

"Look, all we did was hang out together for the afternoon. She saved me from those girls who were trying to strangle me and then we just hung out."

"Doing what?"

"We ate Cronuts and then went to the beach."

Another thing I wish I'd thought about before saying, because . . .

"You ate Cronuts and went to the beach? It's like a scene out of *Grease* or something. The next thing you know, you'll be telling me the two of you sang a song together!"

"We did not sing."

"I don't know. And, like, what was with that other stuff?"

"What other stuff?" There's more?

"On that TV show, before you and Katie 'fell in love'—that reporter was asking her questions and all of a sudden you're all, 'I *love* public transportation! Did I tell you how much I love public transportation? If not, I'll do it again!' Dude, what was up with that?"

I can't answer that question, because if I answer honestly, I'll have to say that my impulse was to save Katie. And I can't give Sandy that kind of ammunition, not when he's got so much already.

"They're going to eat you alive at school tomorrow," Sandy says.

"What do you mean?"

"If they gave you a hard time after Katie called you a wimp, imagine what people will say now that you're Mr. I Love Public Transportation and Mr. I Need a Chick to Save Me from Other Chicks?"

Just then, Stella comes flying down the stairs, the twins in her wake. Sometimes it's like living with that kids' picture book *Make Way for Ducklings*.

"Mom called for you earlier," Max says.

"She sounded mad," Matt says.

"What did she say?" I shout after them.

"She said to tell you," Stella says, "'Drew, just what do you think you're doing?'"

That can't be good.

I look again at the pictures on Sandy's phone and read some of the comments people have left on the article. Eventually I have to force myself to stop reading the comments because it's just too embarrassingly painful.

I've never given much thought to what it must be like to be a celebrity couple—or a "celebrical" couple—although I never even heard that term before today. People talking about you like they know you, speculating about your life and your every move. Who would want that? I've never wanted that. I still don't want it.

"So." Sandy punches me in the shoulder playfully. "Are you going to see her again?"

Am I?

I look at the pictures again and remember my passionate "Ode to Public Transportation." All I can think is that Sandy is right:

Tomorrow at school they're going to totally eat me alive.

KATIE

So *this* is what it's like to have a successful public appearance on national television!

It all begins as I'm standing in the plush carpeted hallway at Willfield Academy, studying the announcements board. There's going to be a mock presidential election in a few weeks—I know my father will win—and a masquerade ball to benefit some sort of charity. Two important events, scheduled so closely together. Not for the first time, I wonder why everything always seems to happen all at once. But then I realize it doesn't matter, since I won't be going to the masquerade ball. I never go to any of the school dances. I never have a date and no one asks me to go as just friends. At least I know my father will win the mock election—eye on the prize!

As I turn away from the announcements board, notebooks held tight against my chest, I smack into somebody.

"Oof, I'm sorry," I say, looking up into the face of Amanda Jamieson, the most popular girl at Willfield Academy. Amanda is incredibly tall, and in her spare time, when she's not being just another mild-mannered student, she is a cover girl for teen magazines.

"I'm sorry," I say again. "Was I in your way?" I'm not sure how I could be, since I'm about a foot shorter than she is, but I start to go around her anyway. That's when I feel a hand on my arm, stopping me. I look at the owner of the hand, but it's not Amanda. It's Deirdre Lowell. That's when I notice that there's a whole bunch of other girls haloed around me.

"No," Amanda speaks. "I just wanted to talk to you?"

I turn around, because I'm sure she can't be talking to me, but of course the only thing behind me is the announcements board.

I turn back to face her, hooking a thumb at my own chest. "Me?" I ask.

And then it hits me, what this is about.

I may not have a lot of direct experience talking to or deal-ing with kids my own age, but I have certainly seen my share of TV programs. So I know that a group of tall popular kids sur-rounding a shorter unpopular kid can only mean one thing:

They're going to shake me down for lunch money!

But wait. Willfield Academy doesn't even have a paid lunch program. I mean, of course people have to pay for it—as my father always says, "There's no such thing as a free lunch!"—but lunch is included as a line item in the tuition. Still, if shake-down money is what they want . . .

Amanda bends down slightly so her made-up face is just inches from mine. I'm about to tell her that I'll gladly have

Kent go get my checkbook, since I don't have any funds on me at the moment, but before I can, she speaks again.

"So, tell me, Katie—"

She knows my name?

"—what's he really like?"

"He?" I'm stumped. This was not what I expected at all. "He who?"

Before Amanda can even answer, though—and this in itself is an unprecedented event, people talking right over Amanda—the others start in so fast and furious with questions and comments that at first I can't make heads or tails of them.

"Sooooooo *cute!*"

"So *hot!*"

"That hair!"

"Those eyes!"

"The way he stood up for you!"

"'I *love* public transportation!'"

Like I say, it takes me a while to catch on, but that last is a dead giveaway.

"Are you talking about *Drew*?" I ask.

"Of course, silly!" Amanda says. "Who else would we be talking about?" She leans in closer. "So, tell me—what's he *really* like?"

I am thankfully saved by the bell.

"Nice?" I respond as I scoot around her, force my way through the throng, and head off to first period.

• • •

By the time I get to first period, I'm almost used to the attention, since Amanda and her group of friends follow me there, peppering me with questions that I don't have a clue how to answer. I'm not surprised when the girls in my class follow suit until the teacher calls the room to order.

I *am* surprised, though, when the boy who sits to the left of me, who has never spoken one word to me, passes me a folded note. I open it to see:

Never been kissed before! I can solve that for you.

I look over and the boy is grinning widely and waggling his eyebrows at me . . . *suggestively.*

How unpleasant.

"No, thank you," I whisper across the aisle. "I'm good."

Lunch brings more surprises. Usually, I spend lunchtime at a table by myself, going over my father's campaign speeches with a red pen in the hopes of finding places where he can improve his message. But today? As soon as I enter the dining hall, there's a groundswell of murmurs rolling in my direction, and I realize that various people are calling for me to sit with them.

Are these people fighting over me?

Before I can choose which way to go, Amanda pulls me down at her table and orders Deirdre to go get me some lunch.

I must say, when my lunch arrives with a second piece of red velvet cake on the tray, a girl could get used to this sort of attention.

The questions they ask me are pretty much the same things they've been asking all day, which basically all boil down to: What is Drew Reilly really like?

The truth is, though, I don't know what he's really like, although I wish I did. And the only answer I've got to give is: Nice. Of course, I do have some other opinions about him, but as flattering as all this attention is, I do not think this is the place to share them.

"Come on, Katie!" Amanda presses. "You've got to give me better than *nice*!"

"Could you introduce me to him?" one of the others asks.

"I highly doubt it," I say, a part of me feeling bad that I can't give them what they want.

"That's a little selfish." The girl sniffs. "Don't you think maybe you could share him a bit?"

Share him?

"It's just that I don't think I'll be seeing him again," I say.

They look at me like I'm crazy.

"He stood up for me," I explain, "and I saved him from a gaggle of girls, and then we shared a limo ride. But that's it. There's nothing more to say. He seemed . . . *nice*."

I feel relieved to get all that out there. As flattering as the attention was in the beginning, it's already starting to feel oppressive.

"Okay. Gotcha." Amanda turns to the others. It's like a switch has been turned off, like instantly I'm no longer there, like they never courted my company in the first place.

"You know what I think?" Amanda asks Deirdre. "I think it'll be *amazing* to have a hot guy our own age living in the White House for once. Like, when has that ever happened?"

"Never," Deirdre says, "at least not in our lifetimes."

"It will be so cool," Amanda says. "Drew is just so hot."

Wait. I stare at my second piece of red velvet cake. They all think Drew's mother is going to *win*? I go into an internal panic but almost immediately I'm able to push the panic aside. These girls just want to see Drew Reilly living in the White House. They're, I don't know, hoping for big photo spreads of him in supermarket magazines, lounging around the Rose Garden in skateboard shorts and nothing else. (I must admit, just picturing that in my own mind, Drew with no shirt on, is making this school uniform feel a little too warm.) So that's what this is really about—no one actually expects her to win!

DREW

Here's the thing.

I've never been the kind of guy bothered overmuch by the opinions of others.

Still, there are times that stuff happens and you think: I may not care what other people think, but I don't want them to think I'm a dork.

Like, take the time I was eight. Sandy and I decided to be Martians for Halloween, which was fine until the green dye we'd put in our hair did not wash out immediately like the tube had promised. My mom, growing frustrated after the third washing, eventually had my dad just buzz all my hair off. But when I looked in the mirror, I started to cry. There are people—Dwayne "the Rock" Johnson and that guy from that old *Breaking Bad* show among them—who can totally rock the bald look. But turns out that, underneath all this hair, I have a very strangely shaped head. Did I want to go to school and hear everybody ridicule me? Absolutely not. Did I want to cover up all the mirrors in our tiny apartment and hide under the bed until my hair grew entirely back? I most certainly did.

But my mom wouldn't let me. She said, and I quote, "Just wear it proudly, Drew. If you go in there scared, of course people will eat you alive." (There's that phrase again.) "But if you stand tall, if you *own* it, if you act like 'I totally meant to do this,' you'll be fine. And if anyone gives you the side-eye, you tell them you had this done in New York City, that it's the latest thing."

I actually started laughing at that last part. Like, what did she think? That people would believe that a shaved head was some kind of sophisticated fashion trend requiring a top-notch salon? Still, her advice served me well. I just behaved all casual, like, hey, I meant to do that, and things at school were totally okay. That was the thing about my mom back then. Before the money and the race, when she and my dad were still around a lot of the time: she actually had some good stuff to say. I don't know, she was just *there*.

But she's not there on Friday morning, the day after my disastrous *That Morning Show* appearance. Is she in Iowa? Delaware? Maybe Kentucky? Who cares where she is, she's not here. There's no one here to give me a pep talk before school, no one to remind me to just stand tall. And I could sure use a boost right now. Because in my head, all I keep seeing is those pictures of me looking like a half-strangled moron and that new GIF Sandy showed me that's making the rounds. The one with me saying, "I just *love* public transportation!" into, like, infinity. So the only person I have to tell me to stand tall as I walk into school is me. Yet, rather than encouraging words, all I can hear is Sandy saying: "They're going to eat you alive."

Except, it's not like that at all.

And in case I need to spell this out, let me just say for the record: no one eats me alive.

Or at least not in the way I imagined.

Sure, some of the guys razz me. But the girls?

"Drew, I loved the way you stood up for Katie!"

"Drew, you're such a good guy!"

"Drew, you're so chivalrous!"

The worst of the bunch?

Millicent.

"Drew, what you did was so romantic—it's like something out of *Romeo and Juliet*!"

Barf. What is wrong with these people?

They trail me around all day, all moony-eyed.

I think I liked it better when people were calling me a wimp.

"Dude," Sandy says, "you could like have any girl in this place with just a flick of your wrist."

"I don't want that!"

"What are you, crazy?"

I don't know. Am I? Is it crazy not to want people paying attention to you for all the wrong reasons?

And I mean, what's so special about what I did? That TV lady totally ambushed Katie. Wouldn't anyone in my position do the same thing? The look on Katie's face. Wouldn't anyone do whatever it took to protect her, to make that sad look go away?

I think I liked Millicent better when she was being rude to me.

What I really liked better was when no one was paying attention to me at all. Because whatever these people think I am, the way they're acting toward me . . . none of it is real.

More than that, I don't know another person who knows what it's like to be in this exact fishbowl . . . except Katie. Which, strangely, makes me want to call her. Of course I know I can't call her. I mean, I really, *really* can't call her. Because that would be crazy, right? But the memory of her at the beach, the wind blowing through her hair . . . The memory of what she looks like when she laughs . . .

On the bus ride home, at least, Sandy's got some words of wisdom for me.

"Just don't feed the beast," he says. "So long as you never see that girl again alone, this'll all die down. Lie low, and something else'll happen to replace you. Because the American public these days? We've got the attention span of gnats."

When I get home, in an effort to take my mind off things, I whip off the tarp on my '63 Corvair.

As I work, my mind goes back to the day and how bizarre everyone acted. And from there, my mind goes to Katie. I think about how in some ways, her lack of knowledge about basic things—like having friends—makes her seem like a visitor from another planet. I think that that's something I'd like to show her: how to have a friend.

Despite her peculiarities, there's something real about her. The girls at school only care about popularity and the surfaces of things. Sure, right now they're all acting like I'm the coolest thing since fast food, but if someone had decided that what I did was *uncool*, they would have all fallen in line with that instead, no matter what they really thought. But Katie's reactions, even if she's kind of screwy in her mono-vision, are somehow genuine. And at least she *has* something she cares about deeply for the thing itself and not because of what anyone else thinks: this stupid election.

Enough. I need to *stop* thinking about Katie. I mean, it's crazy, isn't it? Expending so much mental energy on this strange girl?

But in the end, I can't stop. I think about Katie through dinner and TV watching and even dream about her. When I wake up in the morning, I realize that I have no other choice:

I have to do something about it.

KATIE

In the midst of my dream, I hear a peculiar ringing. *What is that?* It's unlike anything I've heard before. Feeling the security of Dog curled up near my feet, I stretch myself awake, only to find that the ringing is still there. Wait. Did I listen to my iPod too loudly last night? Do I have tinnitus? I hope not. A new malady is *not* in my campaign plans. Plus, it will be very annoying if on Inauguration Day in January, when millions are on the mall cheering for my father, instead of clapping all I can hear is a stupid ringing in my ears.

But then suddenly it stops.

And into the silent void, I hear Cook shout up:

"Miss Katie! Telephone!"

I'm so excited that I leap from the bed, tumbling poor Dog tail over furry head in the process.

"Sorry, Dog!" I shout back at him, racing from the room and down the stairs in bare feet.

The phone for me! It's probably my father with an update on the campaign!

But as I skid to a stop in front of Cook, I see she's holding a thick oblong object pointed at me.

"What's that?" I say.

"The phone." She waves it at me.

"Uh-uh. That's not a phone."

She rolls her eyes at me. "It's the landline. Your daddy keeps it so that his staff can get ahold of him anytime of the day or night, even at home."

"Then how come I've never heard it ring before?"

"You know everybody's on the e-mail these days."

"Everybody's on the e-mail?" Cook is prone to exaggeration. She also has a tendency to put too much oregano in her red sauce. It's all I can do not to roll my eyes right back at her. "The e-mail"—Cook's almost as bad as my father with "the You-Tube." Sometimes I feel like I'm the only person in this house living in the twenty-first century.

Then I remember . . .

The phone! It's for me!

"Who is it?" I ask.

"How should I know?" Cook counters. "Whoever it is, he's probably hung up by now since it's taking you so long to answer."

He? There's a *he* on the other end of the line?

I snatch the unfamiliar object out of Cook's hand, and scarcely able to breathe, intone the important word that begins almost every important exchange in life:

"Hello?"

"Um, Katie?"

"Who is speaking?"

"It's Drew."

"Drew?"

I did not see *that* coming!

But wait a second. "How did you get this number?" I ask. "I don't even know it!"

"Um . . ." He sounds embarrassed. "Turns out, Secret Service agents are good for something. I talked to Clint, the agent assigned to the twins?" He clears his throat. "Anyway, listen. I was wondering . . ."

When nothing follows, I prompt, "I'm listening!" Just in case he doesn't understand that, of course, I am listening.

"Do you want to come over today?"

"Do I want to . . ."

"Just, you know, to hang out? I'm—"

"YES!"

From the way that Cook takes a little leap backward, it occurs to me that maybe my response was too forceful. I've read some books, and if memory serves me correctly, when the heroine is invited out for a social occasion, she never screams her assent. Perhaps, I should have played it more coy? Oh, well. I shrug. Too late for that now. And besides, I'm too excited at the prospect of "hanging out." If depictions on TV programs are correct, and I see no reason to doubt that they are, hanging out is something that all the normal teens are doing these days.

"Um, great," he says.

He sure says "um" a lot. I hadn't noticed that about him before.

"When were you thinking?" I ask.

"Um, today?"

"Right, but when? Lunchtime? After dinner? Perhaps tea-time?"

"How about in two hours?"

"Got it. Two hours."

"But no suits," he adds quickly.

"No suits?"

"Yeah, it's Saturday and I'll be working on my car, so I don't think you'll want to wear one of your business suits for that. You should probably wear something more casual."

"More casual? To work on a car? And we'll be . . . hanging out?"

"Um, yeah."

"YES!" And then, taking the phone away from my ear, I scream, *"KENT!"* because if I only have two hours, there are a *lot* of things I need to do first. Only I forget to push the button to formally end the call before screaming for my Secret Service agent.

Oh, well.

Drew probably didn't even notice. Right?

DREW

What did I just get myself into?

KATIE

"Kent," I say, now that the phone has been safely turned off and my Secret Service agent is before me, "we need to go shopping."

"Oh, you need some new suits?"

"No. I don't need any new suits. I think what I need is something more on the order of"—I almost can't believe this word is about to pop out of my mouth—"*jeans*."

Then I realize I am still wearing my pajamas, so I hurry upstairs to brush my teeth and change my clothes.

And what do I put on to go shopping for something more casual?

A suit, of course.

"*The mall?*" I say to Kent.

"Don't sound so aghast."

"I'm not. I'm just . . . surprised, I guess."

"Well, you did say that your usual tailor probably wouldn't be the way to go today, so . . ."

Once we are in the disappointingly two-story teenage consumer mecca with its plethora of unfamiliar shops, I am frankly at a loss as to which way to turn.

Really. I'm completely stuck standing in place here.

I mean, I've seen kids in casual attire on TV and of course I've seen what the others wear on dress-down days at Willfield Academy, but . . . can this possibly be *right*?

"Kent," I say. "Help a girl out here?"

"Okay, but where are you going that you need jeans for?"

Prior to answering, I twist the fingers of one hand against the fingers of the other in a physical gesture that one should never attempt on national television, because it is a sure "tell" of nervousness and not one I'm accustomed to making.

"Drew Reilly's house?" I whisper as I wince.

"What did you—"

"Drew Reilly's house!" I say more forcefully, causing passersby to stare.

Okay, I'm going to have to watch that.

"I thought that's what you said." Kent shakes his head. "Your father's not going to like this."

"And that's why you're not going to tell him," I say, still forcefully, but, you know, more quietly this time.

"I can't not tell him."

"Yes, you can. I mean, you can not . . . Oh, you know what I mean."

"Right. And I can't do that."

"Tell me, Kent: Who do you work for?"

"The United States government."

"Fine." I roll my eyes at him. "But whose safety are you responsible for?"

"Yours."

"Exactly. And when was the last time I was invited anywhere that wasn't an event at school that everyone else was expected to attend too?"

"In the short time I've known you?"

I nod.

"Never?"

"Exactly again." I sigh. "Please don't spoil this for me, Kent."

"Your father wouldn't like it."

"I know," I say, but the truth is, I don't know that at all. If my father knew where I was going today and who I'd be with, he'd expect me to give him all the intel afterward. And even though I've never had a friend before, at least not one of my own species, I know enough to know that after meeting with your friend you don't go tell your dad everything that was said so he can find things to use as ammunition in his campaign against your friend's mother.

As much as I want my father to win, I also want to know what it's like to have a friend, to be normal, even if just for one day.

And that's when the truth hits me.

"It's just one day, Kent. I'll probably say something stupid or do something stupid and then Drew won't want to hang out with me a second time. Just let me have this one day."

Kent eyes me skeptically for so long that I become convinced he's going to say no, that there's no other way around it, that he just has to tell my father.

"Wellll . . ." He drags out the word. "All right . . ."

I'm so ecstatic, I hug him.

"But if this gets to be a problem," Kent says, "if anything happens that your dad truly needs to know . . ."

"Of course," I promise. "Of course!"

I am positively overwhelmed by the array of jeans in the shop that Kent brings me to, since the last time I owned a pair was back during the first term of Bush II. All I can see is a sea of denim. But as much as I want to just scream, "Kent! Help!," I'm insecure about my neophyte status in the contemporary fashion hierarchy. So I just wade through the racks and stacks until I emerge with something I think *just* might be the ticket.

My feeling of success rapidly fades, however, when I hold the lucky pair up to my body only to have Kent snort at me in derision.

"What's wrong with these?" I ask, wounded.

"Nothing," he says, "if you want to look like Obama that time he threw out the first pitch at a major league baseball game and all the headlines taunted, 'Mom Jeans!'"

I could be wrong, but I'm getting the impression that even though Mom, apple pie, and Chevrolet are considered to be good and all-American things, Mom Jeans are not.

I go back to my flipping through racks and rifling of stacks, but am at a loss to find another pair as exquisite as the first

I picked out. I'm nearly at the end of my tether when Kent asks, "How much time did you say we have?"

I consult my watch. "About forty-five minutes left now."

Kent shakes his head in what can only be termed a "what a hopeless case" shake.

"You do better, then," I dare him.

It takes him about two seconds to whip out a pair and hold them out to me.

"Really?" I say, regarding the jeans. They have an impossibly low waist and even more impossibly narrow legs, and the blue is faded enough to be almost white.

"They're called skinny jeans," Kent informs me.

"Well, I should think so." I pause. "And they typically come with the holes already in them?" There are several slashes in the thighs of the jeans and I can only imagine that when a person puts them on, skin actually shows through.

"Trust me," he says. "Oh, and you'll need a shirt too. Not much point in getting the jeans if you're just going to wear your navy wool suit jacket with them."

Huh. I hadn't thought about a shirt. Drew never said anything about *a shirt*. But before I can begin to internally panic at the idea of more flipping and rifling, Kent holds a shirt out to me.

I think it's what a person might call a T-shirt, based on the neckline, only it has no sleeves.

"Do sleeves cost extra?" I ask. "Because I can afford it."

I can't believe what I'm seeing. Did the Secret Service agent just roll his eyes at me?

I regard the T-shirt again. It's white and has the words "Vote for Pedro" emblazoned in red on the front.

"Who is Pedro?" I ask, racking my brains. But as far as I can recall, a Pedro has never run for president.

"Trust me," Kent says again. "The boy'll think it's funny. The boy'll think it's cool."

I'm a little shocked at Kent. When did Drew Reilly become "the boy" to him? Still, I'm more than a little tickled at the idea of wearing something cool and head off to the dressing room to try the items on.

"Well, what do you think?" I ask Kent, after emerging a short time later.

"Hmm . . ." He studies me from head to toe, a critical expression on his face. "Jeans: good. Shirt: funny. Size of shirt? Too long, too big somehow."

Without explaining what he's doing, Kent takes the bottom of my T-shirt and twists it into a knot on one side so that, when I look in the closest mirror, I see that the hem now hangs higher and more jauntily on my hips.

A thought occurs to me.

"Kent?" I ask. "Are you a Log Cabin Republican?"

He just laughs. "I thought no one was ever going to ask."

Then he informs me that my navy blue pumps are going to spoil the whole effect, which causes him to lead me to the shoe department. He picks out a pair of something in light gray that he informs me go by the trade name of Converse High-Tops.

When I express delight at the apt naming of this product, Kent laughs some more. "Miss Katie, sometimes it's like you're from another planet. You're definitely someone who should pay *more* attention to TV commercials."

If he weren't being so helpful, I might be offended.

Also, it seems like sound advice.

So we pay for my purchases, which I wear out of the store. When we get to the limo, Kent pulls a utility knife out of his pocket and removes all the price tags that are still attached to the clothes I'm wearing.

As he snips the last one, I admire his knife with its many gadgets. "Ooh, handy!"

Last tag snipped, Kent's still not done with me. He reaches up and dislodges my bun of hair from its pins, arranging the strands to his satisfaction.

"No sense in having the right clothes," he says, "if the hair doesn't match."

And when we finally pull onto Drew's street a short time later, I realize Kent is *still* not done with me because he parks the limo about fifty yards from the driveway.

"Oh!" I say, surprised. "You think it would be best for me to walk the rest of the way?"

"Just get out, Miss Katie," Kent instructs.

And I listen because my Secret Service agent hasn't failed me yet!

Once I join him outside, however, he surprises me by bending down and gathering up some muddy sand from the side of the road.

"Uh, Kent?" I say. "What are you doing?"

I am further perplexed to see Kent take the muddy sand and smear it all around the edges of my new light-gray Converse High-Tops.

"What are you doing?" I ask again.

Kent looks up at me with a smile. "You don't want the boy to think you bought all this today, do you?"

I think Kent is an invaluable font of information. How did I not know that about him before?

And as we both get back into the limo, and Kent drives me the rest of the way to my destination, I think how right he is.

If this is the only chance I get at having a day like this, I don't want to mess it up.

DREW

"Hello? Anybody home?"

The first thing I see are her feet.

Well, her sneakers.

That's because I'm underneath my Corvair, on my back, doing some tinkering. It occurs to me that all anyone looking into the garage can see of me are my own feet, sticking out from beneath the front end of the car. I scoot along on the dolly, sliding out into view.

Whoa! Katie's got normal clothes on and her hair is down. I know I told her to dress casual, but I have to admit: I didn't expect this. Especially not the hair. But I don't know how to tell Katie that she looks incredibly hot right now—how would she take such a thing?—and you can't compliment a girl on a major change in her appearance, because then it only turns things into some defensive version of, Oh, so you're saying

I always looked like garbage before? So I go for the safe comment instead.

"Nice sneaks. You just get 'em?"

Katie looks down at her feet, her toes turning inward as she frowns at her high-tops. "How can you tell?"

Well, I can't tell Katie it's because the tread on the sides look too thick and untouched, like she just put them on for the first time a minute ago and then quickly dragged them through the mud to get a worn-these-forever look, can I? She'll just analyze it to death. *She'll* realize that *I* realized that she just got this outfit today and then she'll worry that I think she's trying too hard, which I do think but which I also think is just *incredibly* cute, but I can't tell her that last part because then she'll know I think she's cute and—okay, so maybe I'm the one analyzing this to death. So instead I go with:

"They look great. Can you hand me that wrench over there?"

Katie looks down at me—I imagine my own jeans and T-shirt are covered in grease stains and my work boots are definitely not new—and then looks at the car. A surprised look comes over her face followed by some kind of dawning comprehension.

"Ohhh," she says.

"Oh, what?"

"When you invited me over to work on your car, it wasn't a euphemism."

"A euphemism?"

"The substitution of an agreeable or inoffensive expression when what the speaker means is something else," she says.

For about the millionth time in the short period I've known this girl, the stray thought occurs to me: Why is she so maddeningly annoying?

"I know what the word means," I say with some heat. "But why would I ask you to come work on the car if I meant something else?" To illustrate my point, I reiterate my request: "Could you hand me that wrench from over there?"

A simple request should be followed by simple compliance, right? But as she roots around in the array of tools spread out on the floor, the perplexed expression on her face deepening by the minute, I realize a little more explanation is in order.

So I supply a complete description of what a wrench looks like, causing a lightbulb to go on in her eyes. Just as I inwardly ask myself yet again just why I ever thought this was a good idea, she locates the wrench and hands it to me. As our hands briefly touch, I feel a jolt of what can only be described—no euphemisms needed—as physical lightning.

And all of that, in less than a minute, encapsulates the entire experience of being with Katie.

But that's something else I don't want to say out loud either. And yet I wish I could; it's so frustrating feeling something that strong and not being able to acknowledge it to the other person. I glance at her quickly to see if she feels what I feel right now: Does she? She's so hard to read. Exasperated, I slide back under the car to tinker with this and that.

"Well, this is fun," her voice trickles down to me.

"I'm glad you're having a good time," I call out.

I did tell her in advance what we would be doing. How am I supposed to concentrate on what I need to do if all I can think about is her out there, staring down at my feet? And how am I supposed to concentrate on what I need to do when all I can think about is her, period? I resolve to do my best. I start to whistle. In fact, I almost convince myself that it's just me here, working on my car like any other Saturday, when she finally speaks again.

"So, *this* is what it's like to have a hobby!" she says. I'm so shocked that I forget where I am and sit up too quickly, banging my head hard against the undercarriage of the car.

I slide out, rubbing the quickly forming egg on my forehead.

"Oh, did you hurt yourself?" she asks.

"I don't think this is going to work," I say.

And now she's clearly hurt as evidenced by her guarded, "You want me to go already? No more hanging out?"

"No." I gesture back at the Corvair. "I mean working on the car—maybe it's not the best day for that. Hey, how about getting us a couple of cans of soda from the refrigerator?"

"The refrigerator?"

"You know, something that refrigerates? Especially a room or appliance for keeping food or other items cool? Fun fact: the word 'refrigerator' was first used in 1611, but refrigerators for home use weren't invented until 1913. Okay, I guess that's two fun facts."

She stares at me for a long minute and then breaks into a smile. "I get it! You defined a refrigerator, because of before when I defined 'euphemism' . . ." Her smile widens. "It's like we're two people trading barbs!"

It's all I can do not to roll my eyes.

Okay, I do roll them.

"Yes, Katie, we're like two people trading barbs."

"Oh my gosh, we're *bantering*!"

Another eye roll, only this time I can't help but smile too. "Yes, Katie, we're bantering. Now, about those sodas . . ."

She manages to locate the fridge without further direction, opens it without instruction, and extracts two cans of orange soda. She whips around, pleased with her success. "Glasses?"

"Nah, let's rough it," I say, rising, taking one can from her, flipping the top and handing it back to her, and taking the other can for myself. I flip that top too, clink the can against hers. "Cheers."

She looks around for somewhere to sit and I indicate the workbench. When she fails to do anything, I hop up—a neat athletic execution with no hands needed, if I do say so myself— and indicate the space beside me.

She does what I did, landing with a delicate plop. "Oh!" Again she's pleased.

I shake my head and take a swig of my soda.

She follows suit. Then: "Ooh, fizzy!"

I would shake my head again but there's only so many times you can do that during a social encounter before it starts provoking comment.

But in the absence of a response, a conversational lull falls over us, which Katie breaks with:

"Well . . . this is fun!" And her other old reliable: "So, *this* is what it's like to have a hobby!"

"You've got a hobby," I point out.

"I do?"

"Sure. *Politics*. Isn't that like your main thing?"

"*Politics*. You say that like it's a dirty word."

I snort. "Well, isn't it?"

"What exactly do you think politics is, Drew?"

"Uh, I don't know." I mean, duh. "A chance for fat cats to gather large campaign donations based on idle promises to make changes they'll never fulfill?"

Now it's her turn to snort, only coming from her it sounds more like, "HA!" Followed by: "Look around yourself, Drew."

"What's that supposed to mean?"

"Where you live—in case you haven't noticed, you're one of the fat cats now."

"No, that's—"

"And anyway, politics is wonderful. It's fascinating!"

"Yeah, right."

"It's an opportunity for good men—and women!—to create positive change for people. Even local politics is important. Take my father, for instance. In his first congressional term, a woman who was having a problem with her hospital called his office. She had a baby, hadn't had insurance to cover the delivery, and she was sure the hospital was overcharging her for all kinds of services she never used."

"So, what—your dad went after the hospital for her?"

"No, he had someone on his staff do it."

"HA!"

"No," she says with scorn, "there's no 'HA!' in that. Part of being a good politician is knowing how to delegate. The bottom line is getting things done, serving the will and the good of the people, whatever it takes. And presidential politics is simply that on a far larger scale—the opportunity to make positive changes in the world."

"Right. Like that's what your dad—a *Republican*—is going to do if he gets elected. He's going to be all about 'making positive changes in the world.'"

I have to say that even I find my extensive air quotes there a tad bit annoying. And Katie does too.

"Ohhhh . . . grow up."

"Excuse me?"

"I suppose you're one of those Democrats who thinks that Republicans all have horns growing out of their foreheads?"

I shrug, take another swig of my soda. I could say, If the shoe fits . . . But that would be a snotty thing to say to a guest—a guest who, I must remind myself, I invited here because I felt bad for her that she's never known what it's like to have friends. And because I'm intrigued by her.

And anyway, I'm pretty sure those words are implied.

"Well," she says, "we don't. Or if we do, then Democrats do too."

"Meaning?"

"Yes, there are Republicans who are against social change and for big business, and yes, there are Democrats who tax and spend and would be happy if the whole country went Socialist. But mostly?"

"Yes?" I prompt. "Mostly?"

"In any given presidential election in this country, frequently there's really not much daylight between the major party candidates on most issues. Really, Drew. You should look at your mom's platform, then look at my father's. They're not extremes, they're both the center, and they both want to accomplish pretty much the same things. Sometimes they just word it in different ways."

"That is so much worse!"

"Worse? What are you talking about?"

"That means that when they're campaigning, they're saying all kinds of things just to *appear* a certain way to their . . . *constituencies*, just to get *votes*. But in reality, you say, they're kind of the same?"

Now it's her turn to roll her eyes, shake her head, and snort—and, somehow, she manages to do all three at once.

Which, when you think about it, is almost as impressive a feat as my neat no-hands vertical jump onto the workbench was earlier.

"Be cynical all your life if you want to, Drew, but I prefer to take the idealist approach. And while our electoral system may be intensely flawed, for now, it's the only one we've got."

I would so love to just snort at her some more and laugh in her face but the truth is, when I look at her, I see that she actually *believes* in something. Her green eyes are so intense. Maybe her ideas are twisted, maybe she's nuts—which I think might be a distinct possibility—but the truth of the matter is, where most of the kids I know only care about what their next text message is going to say, Katie believes in something bigger.

I don't know. I think this might be cool. It is, right?

"Look at their platforms," she tells me again, "and then tell me where the big differences lie."

"Yeah," I say, not really wanting to . . . *cede* anything, "maybe I'll just do that."

Like he timed his entrance, my dog trots into the garage, breaking the tension between us.

"Hey, Bowser!" I say.

Katie laughs.

I turn to her. "What?"

"Your dog is named *Bowser*?"

"You have a cat named *Dog* and you're laughing at *Bowser*?"

And suddenly we are both laughing. Into the space that follows, I say: "Tell me something no one else knows about you."

"Excuse me?"

"Everyone knows that you love politics. It's what you've been about your whole life. Tell me something no one knows."

"But I've already talked so much already. Believe me—all those words I just spoke? Unless I'm giving a campaign speech that is a *lot* of words for me to say out loud."

Crazy girl.

"You go first," she says.

"Me?"

"Yes. Tell me something about you that no one else in the world knows."

And for some insane reason I do. I open my mouth and the words just come out:

"My dad is having an affair."

KATIE

I've read the words before in books—"He was dumbstruck" or "She was dumbstruck" or even "They were dumbstruck"—but I don't think it's ever happened to me before. And now I am. I feel struck by what Drew has said and it causes me to go dumb.

But I don't stay that way for long.

"That can't be true!" I blurt out.

And if I was momentarily struck dumb, Drew is positively horrified. Then he does something even more surprising. He laughs.

"HA!" he barks. "Fooled you. You should see the look on your face!"

Well, if I had a mirror handy right now, I could. But since I don't . . .

"I can't believe you bought that!" He laughs. "Can you imagine? I mean, seriously. If that was true, why would *I* ever tell *you*?"

I force myself to laugh along with him. "Right!" I say. "Of course you were just kidding!" This must be what friends do: they kid each other. But I'm tempted to say that line from *Hamlet*, "Methinks thou dost protest too much," only one, that doesn't seem like the kind of thing your average normal teen would say to another average normal teen in the midst of a conversation, and two, I remember my teacher saying when we read the play in school last year that that's the way people always *think* the line goes when in reality it's "The lady doth protest too much, methinks."

And I don't think Drew would like it if I called him a lady.

"Methinks" probably wouldn't go over too well either.

At any rate, this lady thinks that Drew is protesting too much with all his loud laughter.

"Good one!" I laugh some more. "You really had me going for a second there—maybe even a whole minute! There's just one problem."

"What's that?"

I stop laughing. "You weren't kidding, were you?"

All of Drew's attempts at false cheeriness collapse and he just groans.

"Why did I have to say that out loud?" he says, squeezing his eyes shut angrily as he strikes the heel of his palm against his forehead.

I'm tempted to tell him this won't work. Believe me, I've struck my forehead with the heel of my palm before and it does no good. At best, there's a slight jarring sensation; and at worst, you wind up with one heck of a bruise.

"It's okay," I say.

He looks at me like I'm nuts. "How can it possibly be okay?"

"Well, not the affair part. Obviously. If it's true." I think about the words he's said and his own reaction after saying them, and it hits me what he's most worried about. "But if you're worried that because of who I am, I'll turn around and tell my father, that won't happen."

I say the words just to put his mind at ease, but as soon as they're out of my mouth, I realize something surprising: they're actually true.

If anyone asked me when I got up this morning, or on any other previous day in my life, what I'd do if any information fell into my hands that might help my father with his campaign, I'd answer in the popular teen vernacular: "*Duh!* Of *course*, I'd run and tell him!" But Drew didn't tell me what he said as though he was talking to Edward Willfield's daughter. He said it like he was confiding in a friend. I don't think in my whole life anyone's ever confided something in me as a friend before. Does Cook confessing her fears about what would happen that one time Sonny found out that Ava shot Connie on *General Hospital* count? I don't think so.

I try to think what I've seen characters on TV do in similar situations and I come up with something.

I place my hand on Drew's bicep and try to ignore how good it feels against my hand. It's such a heady feeling, that simple physical contact, and my heart races a little faster. I wonder if I'm going to pass out. But I force myself to concentrate on his problem and what he's going through. I wait until he finally looks up, his eyes meeting mine, to say: "Tell me. What's going on?"

Then I shut up and listen.

"Sometimes I think it all started when we struck it rich." Drew looks around him in disgust. Since we're only in the garage, I deduce that his disgust is reserved for the large house attached to the garage and everything that goes with it.

"I'm not saying that poor is somehow better than rich, or that poor people are happier necessarily. But for us? I think we were. Back then, my parents were both there most of the time when I got home from school. We'd have dinner together, do stuff together, go places together. Then my dad made all that money. And, at first? That was pretty okay too. Instead of just dreaming about the things we wanted, we could go out and buy them. And instead of just going places together, we could go to really nice places, anywhere we wanted. Then my mom decided she wanted to go into politics and for a while, even that was okay. My dad supported her. He said she should do whatever it takes to follow her dream. But then? I don't know. Somewhere along the way, something . . . *happened*. They stopped talking *to* each other and started talking *at* each other. At first, my dad would travel with my mom every single time she went away. Now it seems like he only goes if he absolutely has to, if Ann—my mom's campaign manager—says it'll look bad if he's not there."

He pauses and I simply wait until he's ready to continue. But while I'm waiting, I reach out my hand and lightly take hold of his. He stares at our two hands joined together, as though he's surprised to see them like that, like maybe they belong to other people. Then I feel him thread his fingers through mine so they're twined together and he tightens his grip before continuing. It's hard to concentrate over the distraction of this amazing hand-holding—it's got a life of its own, like the sound of the ocean roaring through my ears—but I force myself to focus.

"I hear them arguing all the time, the rare times they're both at home, but if I walk into the room they just stop. And when I ask them what's going on, they won't tell me. They say everything is fine. Yeah, right!" He laughs harshly. "Oh, and my dad? If I come across him talking on the phone, he quickly says to whoever he's talking to, 'Let me get back to you on that,' and then hangs up. And the worst? Used to be, when he was working on his laptop, he'd sit in this comfy chair he's got in his office, the one piece of furniture left from the old apartment. He'd sit there, his back to the door, and I'd sneak up on him and fake scare him. Of course, when I did, I could see whatever he was working on. But now? He never sits in that chair anymore. He sits behind his desk, facing the door, the back of his laptop blocking the view. He's like some gunslinger in an old Western, always sitting facing the saloon doors so he can see any threat coming his way, so as soon as anyone walks in he can put the top down or change the screen, anything to keep other people from seeing what he's actually doing. Aaargh!"

Drew lets go of my hand and grabs the sides of his head with both hands. "Why am I even telling you all this? I haven't even told Sandy!"

I can't say that I'm not flattered by that last part. Sandy is his best friend.

I try to think of what a TV character might say, given this situation. And I must admit, there's a lot of good material there. But it hits me. If I want to have a friend, if I want to *be* a friend, then I can't just go with the recycled words of TV characters, however good those words might be. I can't even go with the recycled words of Shakespeare. For this to work, I'm going to have to be myself, even though I'm not always sure who that is.

So instead of falling back on the familiar, I reflect on what he's said, and take a mental walk around in his work boots before speaking.

"I think it's obvious why you haven't told Sandy any of this," I say, wondering if I'll ever meet Sandy before concluding probably not.

"It is?"

"Sure. He's your best friend. You grew up together. He knows all these people. Maybe he even thinks of your father as a second father. Whatever your dad may have done, you don't want to tarnish his image in Sandy's eyes. Whatever you're going through now, whatever bad feelings you're having, it's somehow a little bit better—even though the situation stinks—if you can keep your best friend from experiencing those bad feelings too."

"That's exactly what it's like." He stares at me, curious, stunned. "But how did you know that? I didn't even know that and they're my feelings!"

I shrug. "Maybe it's easier to see a situation for what it is when you're not so close to it?"

Hey, that was really good! I mean, of *course* I mean every word I'm saying. It's just exciting to think that maybe I could actually be good at this friend stuff.

Sometimes, I must admit, it's very hard for me to stay in the moment. There's the me that's living, but there's also the me that's always outside myself evaluating, taking a poll on how things are going.

And then I stop myself. Why am I even thinking of polls, however remotely, at a time like this? Why must I analyze myself from the outside? I decide to refocus my energies into trying to be a good friend, into showing Drew that I'm not just listening—I want to help him figure this thing out because I actually care about what he's telling me.

"I'll tell you something else I'm seeing," I say.

"What's that?"

"You *think* you know what's going on with your father. But really? You don't know anything. Not for sure. I mean, of course it looks bad. But what do you have besides a whole lot of circumstantial evidence?"

Another stunned look from him, like this is an idea that hasn't occurred to him before. I'm just full of new ideas today!

"And," I add sagely, "no one is ever found guilty on purely circumstantial evidence."

"That is an entirely false statement," he objects.

"True," I concede. "But if I'd cited percentages instead of saying 'no one,' my argument wouldn't have sounded half as good. When you pontificate about something, even if you know it to be false, never go with the wishy-washy—that's like Politics 101."

He smiles for the first time in what seems like hours.

"Anyway," I say, "it's enough true to apply here. You don't really know anything, not for sure. And even if you did?"

"Even if I did, what?"

"You can't let it bother you."

"What are you talking about?" The smile goes away. "How can you say that?"

I'm beginning to think that being real has inconsistent effects.

"Because your parents aren't you." I can't believe that I, of all people, am saying that. "Whatever is going on, no matter how it looks, it's between them. And whatever's going to happen, it's going to happen anyway, and no amount of worrying on your part can change that. You have to live your own life, Drew, and find a way to just be happy."

DREW

I don't even think about it. I simply close the space between us and place my lips on hers.

KATIE

I'm so stunned, I just sit there, my lips still, not doing anything.

It's like I'm outside my body, looking at myself being kissed. A boy is kissing me. I can't believe I'm being kissed.

After a half minute of me not moving, not responding, Drew pulls away.

"I'm sorry, Kat," he says, "I shouldn't have done that. I don't know what I was thinking."

"No," I say, "it's okay. It's just that . . ."

How do I tell him that nothing like this has ever happened to me before? How do I tell him that this is a moment I've dreamed about countless times—my first kiss—but I'd reached the point where I'd come to accept that it might never happen to me?

"Just that what?" he asks.

"You asked me before to tell you something that no one else knows about me."

"Right. And I wound up telling you about my parents instead."

"Well." I take a deep breath. "That." I point at his lips, touch my own. "People speculate, but no one knows for sure, and I'm telling you: I've never done that before."

"I'm sorry," he begins once more, but this time it's me closing the distance between us.

"Can we try that again?" I ask when I'm just a breath away.

Before he can answer, I touch my lips to his. Only this time? I don't observe myself from outside. Instead, I remain firmly in my body as I experience all the sensations that a kiss, a real kiss, brings.

As I experience the at-first soft and then more urgent sensation of his lips pressing back against mine, I feel his hands touch my cheeks. It's as though he is willing me to remain there, in the moment with him. I slide my arms around his waist, my hands trembling slightly, barely able to believe the feel of his body . . . my fingers separated from his skin only by his T-shirt.

This moment is more than anything I have ever dreamed.

DREW

Kissing Katie is crazy. Not only because of who she is and Sandy's words of wisdom about not being caught alone with her again—but because of how good it feels. We kiss over and over again. I can't help myself. I don't *want* to help myself.

Still, after Katie leaves I tell myself that, while it was a nice afternoon and she was interesting to talk to, it was just a one-time thing and it's time to get back to real life. I tell myself this even though I've never felt what I felt with Katie while kissing any girl before. After the initial awkwardness (and the second and third and fourth kisses), we became like one kissing mind.

The problem is that when I wake up on Sunday morning, I'm still thinking about her (probably because I went to sleep on Saturday night thinking about her) and before my left hand knows what my right is doing, I'm phoning her landline a second time to ask her if she wants to come hang out again and maybe help me work on my car.

It takes two to tango, as the saying goes, and if she were to say no to me, that really would be that.

But she says yes and comes over. We have another really great time and there's more kissing. Oh, *is* there more kissing.

We make a pact not to discuss our parents' campaigns, to not let it affect us, a pact that Katie finds particularly tough to keep. Somehow, though, I don't mind. Politics—it's just a big part of who Katie is.

The next weekend we do it all again.

And the week after that?

I start asking her over every day.

It's all so crazy. It's like, on paper, there's no way this should work. On paper, she's not the girl that anyone would pick to be with me, me included. But that doesn't seem to matter because in real life, she's smart and she's funny and she's even learning how to identify a wrench without too much description first.

She even does this—here comes that word again!—*crazy* stuff that I just totally love. Like, she gets a lot of her ideas about people and teen relationships from TV programs she's seen. So, one time, we're in my garage, she's handing me tools, and she just breaks out into song.

I would never tell her this to her face but, truth time here: girl can't sing. But it's still cute and funny and like nothing any girl has ever done with me before—I mean, there's not even a radio playing to bring this all on—and when she pauses for breath, I can't help myself.

"Kat," I ask, "what are you doing?"

Ever since she confessed "Kat" is the nickname she's always wished people would call her, I've ended up calling her that most of the time.

"Isn't that what people do when they like each other?" she asks.

"Where'd you get that idea?"

She looks wary now as though sensing a trap, either from me or from life. *"High School Musical?"* she asks as much as answers.

I nearly bust out laughing. Did she really just say what I think she said? Could she possibly be serious? But then I see that she is, indeed, dead serious. Suddenly I don't have the heart to tell her that, one, that's a really old movie; two, no, people don't really do that in real life; and three, she can't really sing.

So, barely able to believe what I'm saying, I ask, "How does that song go again?"

Next thing I know, we're doing a duet.

Crazy, right?

It's a good thing, I tell myself, that Sandy isn't here to see this.

But then, no one is, because that's the thing—or just yet another of the many other things in whatever this thing is:

We agree, early on, not to tell a soul.

Well, it's my idea initially and Kat is reluctant—she doesn't like the idea of lying to her father. But then I explain to her that it's not really lying; it's simply not telling, not . . . *offering*. And I further point out how insane people got, not to mention You-Tube and TMZ, when all they had to go on was that stupid little incident with *That Morning Show*.

"Can you imagine what the press would do if they knew about *this*?" I say. "Can you imagine what kind of . . . *fodder* we'd become?"

I'm not even always sure what *this* is. I mean, can it really be called dating if we never go anywhere? But the thing is, I know if we went public, it would be awful. Because while I may not be an expert on relationships, I know there's a little more to it than what you see in *High School Musical*.

I've seen other kids go through it at school. So often, it's the same thing. Person X likes Person Y. And what do you know, it turns out that Person Y likes Person X back. It's a very nice thing. It's the way life should be. But then once all the other letters of the alphabet find out about it, they stick their noses into things—maybe some people think Person Y isn't cool enough for Person X; or maybe some people think things aren't progressing fast enough emotionally or physically and that Person X shouldn't wait on Person Y. Whatever the case, whatever the reasons, relationships that might otherwise have lasted wind up foundering when all the other letters in the alphabet get involved.

I don't think Kat and I are ready for that. This . . . *thing* is just too new to let all the other letters in.

So I find a way to explain all this to Kat, minus the metaphor involving all the letters, and she sees the wisdom of my ways.

Which I must admit is a very flattering thing.

So we agree to keep this to ourselves, at least for now. Neither one of us wants photographers in our faces all the time. Although there are times when I wish I still had my iPhone so I could take my own pictures. Some selfies, not for Instagram or Facebook, but just for myself.

As it is, all I have to rely on is my own imperfect memory. Sometimes, I worry that already I'm forgetting things. So when I lie in bed at night, I run through the day's events in my mind. In a way, it's like having a photo album with an endless series of still shots. There's Kat with orange soda on her shirt because she's laughing so hard at something I said. There's Kat, mouth open wide, singing off-key. There's me, kissing Kat.

So many pictures that no one else gets to see.

Because I don't even tell Sandy. It stinks, keeping such a big secret from my best friend, but one of the perks about best friendship is knowing the other person through and through. If there's one thing I know about Sandy it's that, despite all his good points, the dude does not know how to keep a secret, which is one of the main reasons why I never told him about my dad and his possible cheating on my mom. In fact, the only person who knows about me and Kat is Kat's Secret Service agent, Kent.

So, naturally, disaster has to strike.

We're in the garage when I hear voices coming up the drive, heading our way.

"Oh, no," I say, "it's the twins."

Somehow, we've managed to avoid them the past few weeks. Probably because they're always involved in practice for this, and sport event for that, with rehearsal for who knows what thrown in.

It certainly wasn't like that when I was their age. It was just me and Sandy and whoever else we could rustle up for games outside, back in the old neighborhood. But the twins? They've got Suzuki violin and piano and basketball, not to mention soccer year-round. My dad says if they're not kept busy, trouble results, but I believe what they are is overscheduled. But perhaps I'm old-fashioned. Next thing you know, I'll be telling kids to get off my lawn.

"I'd love to meet them!" Kat says.

"No," I insist, "you really wouldn't, not today. They are the worst blabbermouths in the world."

So without further ado, I take her hands, lower her onto her back on the dolly, and slide her under the Corvair. I know it's not a hugely . . . *dignified* thing to do. But it's the garage. Where else am I going to hide her?

I straighten up just as the twins walk in, Clint behind them.

"Hey, guys!" I say in a too-hearty voice. "How was your day at school? How was, um, violin practice?"

"It's Tuesday," Max says. "We don't have violin on Tuesday."

"We have soccer," Matt says.

"Right, right," I say, looking down at their feet: cleats. "Of course. How was that?"

I should never have looked down at their feet because no sooner does Max say "It was fine" than Matt points.

"Who's that under your car?"

"Sandy!" I say, too loudly, the first thing that pops into my head. Also, it's logical, right?

"Nuh-uh." Matt shakes his head.

"What do you mean, nuh-uh? Of course it's Sandy!"

"Nuh-uh," Matt says again, still pointing at the incriminatingly small Converse High-Tops.

Kat is what you call petite (something I love about her) with feet to match (which I also love), but right now those petite feet are working against us.

"Those are *girls'* feet," Matt persists. "Do you have a *girl* under there?"

Thinking fast, I pull the boys into a huddle and whisper to make it look good.

"Shh!" I say. "Do you want him to hear you? Haven't you noticed before that Sandy has little-girl feet? He's very sensitive about them."

The twins stare back at me.

So I appeal to their sense of empathy, such as it is. "How would you like it, if you had girls' feet and people were always calling attention to them? You would totally hate that, right?"

I feel guilty even as I'm saying it. If there's one thing I've learned from Kat, it's that people are always telling guys "You do X like a girl" or "You do Y like a girl" like it's some kind of huge insult, but there's no equivalent reverse. If you tell a girl she shoots hoops like a guy, it's a compliment.

But I don't have time to consider language and gender politics right now because the twins, who genuinely like Sandy, look ashamed.

"Hey, don't worry about it," I say, gently pushing them out of the garage as Clint gives me a suspicious look I totally ignore. "I'll find a way to make it up to Sandy. He's very sensitive but his memory stinks. He'll forget about this by morning."

Then I slide the garage door down and lock it from the inside.

Once they're gone, I quickly slide Kat out from under the car. I expect her to be mad because, one, I used "girls' feet" as an insult, and two, her clothes are now covered with grease from being under the Corvair.

But she's too busy laughing to be mad.

She sits up on the dolly, staring at her own feet. "To think that, of all things, we were almost done in by my feet!" She laughs some more.

I'd like to join her, but I can't because suddenly I'm mad at the world.

"What's wrong?" she says. "Do you want to bindi the car?"

"It's Bondo," I say. "You Bondo a car. It's this stuff you use to fill in dents and dings so that later when you paint it, you get a smooth finish. Bindi is . . . something else."

"What's wrong?" she asks again.

"I just wish . . ."

"You wish what?"

"As great as all this is," I gesture ruefully at the garage, "sometimes I just wish we could be a little more normal, you know? Like go out in public together, just once, on a real date like other couples. I'd just like to be able to take you some-where."

"Where would you take me?"

I go through all the usual suspects. "Dinner? A movie?"

Kat looks at me wistfully. "That would be nice."

She's quiet for a long moment. We both are. But before long, her expression brightens.

She tells me she has an idea, a terrific idea.

"I know somewhere we can go," she says.

What's Kat come up with?

It's not exactly what you'd call normal, but it *is* public. Rela-tively.

KATIE

The past few weeks with Drew have been the most amazing of my life, even better than the times my father has won elections. All those years I spent keeping my eye on the prize, I had no idea what I was missing. The real prize? Now I think maybe it's living. It's not that I don't care if my father wins the presidential election—I still do, very much so—but it's so nice to finally have a boyfriend. It may be even nicer to simply have a friend. (Actually they're both great, amazing even—and in one person!)

One thing Drew and I don't talk about much? The election. Partly because I don't want to hurt his feelings, as I'm sure my father will win. But also, what's the point in talking about something that can only be a source of tension between us? So when we're together, I avoid the topic of the election as much as I can. I try to pretend it doesn't exist, even though the clock is ticking.

Just because we don't talk about the election, however, it doesn't mean we don't talk about politics. Well, I talk about it anyway. It's the one thing I'm an expert on and it continually amazes me how much Drew doesn't know. Come to think of it, I'm also constantly amazed by how little the average American teenager knows about our political process. Those polls with the percentages of high school students saying they can't name the vice president of the United States? Don't even get me started. How depressing! Most people *can* name the president. I must say those who can't really worry me.

So I talk to Drew about your basic stuff: how a bill becomes a law, the history of the filibuster, what Lincoln has to do with the Log Cabin Republicans.

It would probably surprise people to learn: Drew is growing very interested in all these things. At least, when I'm talking he seems to be.

And while I teach him about politics, what does he teach me about?

How to be a friend. How to have a romantic relationship.

So there we were, going along perfectly happy. I had grown used to the fact that our relationship is one hundred percent confined to a garage—like Drew says, who wants the headaches of the paparazzi?—but then he gets upset about the fact that we *are* confined to the garage and we *can't* do anything normal like go on a date in a public place, and *that's* when I come up with my plan.

"Next Friday," I say, "they're having a masquerade ball at my school. It's to benefit some charity."

"I don't see how that solves anything, Kat."

I take a moment to enjoy him calling me Kat again—I just love that!—before going on to state the obvious.

"We could go," I say, and then I add, just in case he doesn't get it yet, "you know, together?"

"How's that going to work? You ever see when people do that in movies?"

Of course I probably have, since I've seen a *lot* of movies. But I'm not sure what he's getting at.

"Probably," I say. "And?"

"They always have two main characters that like each other but don't know it yet or something silly like that. Anyway, they both wind up at a masquerade ball and they both have masks on and then *of course* they wind up dancing together and *of course* their attraction grows, because they're masked and being hidden behind masks they can let their prejudices of the other person go and let their real selves shine through. It's supposed to be so dramatic and cool—he doesn't know it's her! She doesn't know it's really him! But in reality, the whole audience is like, 'Dude, how can you *not* know it's her? It's the same chick—same body, same hair, same eyes and smile—but with a little tiny mask around her eyes!'"

"You have given this a lot of thought."

"Maybe."

"I see what you're saying, but that doesn't really apply here."

"How can it not?"

"Because the Willfield Academy Masquerade Ball isn't really like that."

"How can a masquerade ball be not like a masquerade ball?"

"Willfield Academy just likes fancier names for everything. For example, we never have 'lunch' if we can have a 'luncheon.' Every day, the midday meal is like a special event. And the masquerade ball? It's just a fancier name for costume party. At least that's what I think. I've never actually gone to one of these before."

"So you're saying we'd wear full costumes? Not just silly little masks?"

"Uh-huh."

"Cool! But what would we go as?"

We decide to go as something where our costumes makes some sort of thematic sense together and to be characters from some famous movie. But once we decide those two things, Drew, despite his inordinate fascination with the way masquerade ball scenes are portrayed in film, leaves which film up to me.

I scan my brain for things I've seen recently.

"*Titanic*?" I reject it before he can with "Too tragic." "*Lincoln*?" Another self-rejection from me as I point out, "Mary Todd was kind of a loon."

"Neither of those would be good anyway because," Drew says, "like with the tiny-mask thing, it'd still be our heads on top of the costumes. Too recognizable."

I picture Drew with a Lincoln beard and a stovepipe hat. It's not actually a good image.

"You're right," I concede.

"We really need something more costumey."

"Costumey? Is that even a word?" Before he can respond, I say, "Hey! I've got it!"

"You do?"

"We could go as characters from *The Wizard of Oz*!"

As he thinks about this, I wait for him to come up with something to object to, but after a moment, he smiles. "Cool. I could be the Tin Man. If I have a bunch of silver makeup all over my face, no one will recognize me."

"And I could be Dorothy! I've always wanted ruby slippers. I wonder if they make them with real rubies? And I could get a red wig and maybe break into song—"

"Um, Kat?"

"Hmm . . ." I'm so busy visualizing what this will all be like, it takes me a minute to realize he's no longer smiling. "What's wrong?"

"Cute as you'd look in a little blue-and-white-checked dress, and as, um, *fun* as it might be to see you break into song in public, you as Dorothy won't work."

"You don't think I could be a redhead?"

"That's not it. It's just that, you as Dorothy . . ." He sighs. "It's still not costumey enough. I'm sure the wig would be fine but it would still so obviously be *you* under it."

I'm tempted to be offended but I do see what he means.

"So who else could I be? Not Glinda the Good—there'd be the same problem as with Dorothy. What other major female character could I be that requires a lot of concealing makeup?"

"I've got it!"

I narrow my eyes at him. "You're not going to suggest that I go as the Wicked Witch of the West, are you?"

"Of course not."

That's a relief.

"You should go as Toto."

This requires more than a narrowing of the eyes. It also requires hands on both hips and as much indignation as I can muster. "You want me to go as *the dog*?"

"Everyone loves Toto!"

"You may not have noticed this about me? But I'm a *cat* person."

"Think about it, though . . ."

I don't know. But there's just something about Drew. As much as I want to hold on to feeling indignant, before long . . .

"Sure," I tell him. "I can be Toto."

But no sooner do we get *that* settled and I tell him I'll have Kent pick up costumes for us at the shop in town than Drew says . . .

"Oh, no." He laughs. "It's no good if we buy the costumes. We need to make them."

"Who are you—Martha Stewart? Real people don't *make* their own costumes."

I could be wrong, but this is the closest we've come to having an actual fight since we first kissed. Which, when you think about it, is really amazing. If we're in a fight, I'm sure I'll win—I'm the one with common sense on her side.

"Not everyone just goes out and buys stuff all the time," Drew says, "particularly not items to be worn just once and then put aside."

I'm about to point out to him that, actually, people do this all the time. If he wants, I can put it in an essay and footnote everything.

But then he starts talking about growing up poor, how before his family had money he and his mom used to make his Halloween costumes together because that's all they could afford. This only serves to remind me that I haven't even gone out for Halloween since I was very small, because the fall season has always been reserved in my house for politics. Suddenly, homemade costumes actually sound good.

"Sure," I find myself agreeing, "we could do that."

It never occurred to me before how difficult it would be to make my own dog costume. Of course, that's probably not something that occurs to most people outside of costume designers in Hollywood who just happen to be designing outfits for actors dressed as dogs. Drew, on the other hand, finds making a Tin Man costume a breeze. Maybe it's because he's so handy with working on cars, but before I know it, he gets a bunch of cardboard to fashion into a barrel shape, a funnel for a hat, and sprays it all with silver spray paint. He tells me that on the night of the masquerade ball he'll put silver makeup all over his face. All of the other items, like the funnel, he gets from his supply of stuff in the garage, but the silver makeup he'll order online from a costume retailer.

Like I said, easy.

But me? With the strips of various shades of brown-colored crepe paper? The furry this and the fuzzy that? Not to mention, a *tail*? Let's just say it's a bit of a chaotic mess for a while.

But that's okay because we're doing something in Drew's garage other than bindiing the Corvair and we're doing it together.

And so the week flies by with only a few flies getting in the ointment.

The first fly happens at school. It's not that the masquerade ball has been called off—that would be a true tragedy, but no, I'm able to buy my two tickets for Friday night just fine.

The fly is the mock election, which is held on Thursday.

I walk into school in the morning feeling such a sense of excitement and head straight for the gymnasium, where the mock voting booths are set up. Students have put up signs on the walls lining the corridor leading up to the room. The signs say things like A VOTE FOR EDWARD WILLFIELD IS A VOTE FOR WILLFIELD ACADEMY and SAMANTHA REILLY FOR A BETTER TOMORROW THAN TODAY. I'm sure whoever thought of that last one *thought* it made sense. But personally? I find it grammatically questionable. There's even one sign up for Bix Treadwell, the third-party candidate, that says: BIX TREADWELL: BECAUSE BILLIONAIRES CAN'T BE BOUGHT. Everyone knows Bix doesn't stand a chance. I can only imagine that whoever put it up is some sort of idealist who believes that a third-party candidate can actually win a presidential election. Ha! Not in this century.

I enter the voting booth and pull the lever next to my father's name.

Afterward, I accept my "I voted today!" sticker and proudly stick it to the lapel of my blazer. Over the course of the day I note that every single student I see in classes or pass in the hallways is also sporting the same sticker. I'm filled with pride. Every year, I hear some sort of horror story about the low percentage of voter turnout in American elections.

It is appalling. Willfield Academy, on the other hand, has a history of having one hundred percent turnout for mock elections.

I suppose that may be because it's a requirement, but still.

My school and patriotic fervor soars throughout the day. Honestly, I'm so proud of my father, so proud of my school, so proud of my country—there are no words for it.

By all rights, these soaring feelings should reach crescendo at the all-school assembly held during the final period of the day. This is when the headmaster will read out the election results. This is when my father, in a mock election that is no doubt a harbinger of the real election in just four weeks, will be declared president. After all, Willfield Academy is like the *Weekly Reader* poll—its choices are always right.

One can imagine my horror, then, when what comes out of the headmaster's mouth is: "Samantha Reilly, thirty-nine percent of the vote; Bix Treadwell, thirty-three percent of the vote; Edward Willfield, twenty-six percent of the vote; and the cooking staff, with write-in votes, two percent of the vote." He stares at the sheet of paper, perplexed for a moment, before concluding: "Well, I suppose the cooking staff has upped its game lately. So kudos to them!"

Never mind the cooking staff. What just happened here? How is it possible that my father lost to both Samantha Reilly *and* Bix Treadwell? I suppose I should be grateful that the cooking staff hasn't *upped* their game any more than it has—otherwise, he might have lost to them as well!

All around me, I hear the buzz of whispers. And the only words I'm able to make out? My name. It feels as though every eye in the room is upon me, waiting for a reaction. But I refuse to give them what they want. People in my family are nothing if not stoic. So outwardly, I maintain a look of serenity. I even manage a smile because I refuse to reveal the panic and distress and sheer sadness I feel inside.

I think of Willfield Academy's founding fathers—aka my ancestors—and how they must be rolling in their graves.

How could this have happened? Should I have campaigned harder for my father? Okay, I'll admit I didn't campaign here at all, but that's only because I figured it was implied. I mean, yes, everyone knows that Connecticut leans liberal, and Willfield Academy is traditionally part of that liberal leaning—save the whales and yada yada. But wasn't it safe to assume that, just like once upon a time America went in whatever direction Henry Ford went, that a school that actually bears the name of Willfield would go in the direction of the only candidate that shares that name?

It's only as I'm shoving my way out of the auditorium, noticing the strange smiles on other students' faces as I pass them, that it hits me.

This has nothing to do with my father. Whatever . . . *this* is, this mock election has been engineered with the sole purpose of mocking me. People have deliberately thrown their support in other directions as a vote not against my father, but against me.

I have to admit, that stinks.

It's not like I've ever tried to win any popularity contests before, but still, I don't think that before today I ever realized how much free-floating animosity there is in the world.

Then I look at the bright side. Okay, so maybe nobody around here really likes me, but does that matter? After all, I have Drew.

Then I think of the other bright side. If these mock election results are truly all just one big mock, then they have absolutely *no* bearing on the upcoming real election. They are a harbinger of zip.

And you know what two bright sides make? A whole.

The cooking staff, my foot.

That night, I'm putting the finishing touches on my Toto costume, gluing strips of brown and autumn-hued crepe paper to the shell of a Ted costume I had Kent pick up—you know, Ted, like in the *Ted* movie?—when the second fly flies into my ointment. This one comes in the form of a phone call from my father on Cook's phone.

"Can you believe the latest poll numbers?" he asks without preamble.

Can I? Actually, I can't. Probably because I haven't looked at them this week. And why is that? I've been too busy spending time with Drew.

"The latest numbers are—" I start to say but then stop because I don't know how to finish this sentence. Are the numbers phenomenal? Catastrophic? No, that last can't be true. Maybe the numbers are just . . . numbers?

But apparently it's okay that I don't know how to finish the sentence because my father continues with, "And the worst part is Bix Treadwell."

"Bix?" I say, truly shocked. How can Bix matter? He's just a third-party candidate and a distant third at best.

"This new tactic of his," my father steams. In a mocking tone he adds what is apparently a new campaign slogan of Bix's, "Above the Fray."

"It is kind of catchy," I concede.

"Catchy? Did you just call it catchy?" He sighs. "You're not the only one who thinks so. The press is eating it up, so of course the populace is following suit. You'd think no one ever swore before to run a clean campaign—I do that all the time!"

"True," I say. And it is true. We do that and then we say whatever we want.

"And he's so clever," my father continues. "He *says* that he's running a clean campaign, that he's 'above the fray,' when all the while he's *implying* that Samantha Reilly and I are just a couple of mudslingers. I call that dirty pool, princess. What say you?"

"Definitely dirty pool," I agree.

"Think about it! While claiming to be not slinging mud, what's he doing but slinging more mud?"

"Exactly," I say. Then: "Just how bad *are* the poll numbers?"

There's a sharp intake of breath coming from the other end of the line.

"Baby," my father says, "do you honestly not know?"

"I've just been very busy this week."

"With what?"

"With school."

Well, that's technically true, isn't it? I've been busy with Drew, making costumes for the masquerade ball we're going to tomorrow night, which is at my school—hence, I've been busy with school.

"Well, stop!" my father practically shouts. "Eye on the prize, baby, eye on the prize!"

Let's face it. Parents are confusing. On the one hand, my father says he wants me to have a normal life, while on the other, well, look at him. Clearly, I get my vernacular and life outlook from him.

"Of course," I quickly agree. Then, even though I'm beginning to worry—could that stupid mock election at Willfield Academy actually turn out to be a true harbinger of national sentiment after all?—I hasten to reassure him.

"I'm sure this is just a glitch," I say. "You know the beginning of October is a notoriously fickle time for voters. They're so busy watching the stupid World Series, they don't know what they're telling pollsters! But as soon as the face-to-face debates start next week, the public will see what a superior candidate you are and then this one lousy glitch will just be a bad and distant memory."

"I hope you're right."

"You know I am. Now tell me: How's the campaign trail going otherwise? I hope you're not eating too many extra dinners. You know that extra salt can wreak havoc in terms of facial puffiness when you go before the cameras . . ."

And so we continue for another hour, talking about the same topics we've been covering on a regular basis for most of my life. Not once does my father ask just what it is at school that has had me so busy. Which is a relief, because at least I don't have to lie or sort-of lie to him. Still, it would be nice for a change if he were to show a healthy interest in whatever I might be doing outside of the campaign.

I do feel a bit guilty. Maybe, just like the loss of the Willfield Academy mock election was my fault, I'm also to blame for whatever is going wrong with the polls? Maybe, if I'd kept my eye on the prize like I was supposed to, maybe none of this would be happening?

But then, as we get off the phone and I see my Toto costume, I remember that tomorrow night I'll be going on the first public date of my life and with a boy I actually like.

And it hits me:

For the first time in a long time, maybe the first time ever, I actually want something just for myself.

DREW

It's not often in a guy's life that he gets to have a Cinderella moment: the transformation of dressing up in something wholly different and going someplace to be with a special someone, knowing that when the clock strikes a certain hour it'll all be over with. But that's exactly what's happening tonight. Only in this case the someplace is the masquerade ball at Kat's school and the ending won't be at the traditional fairy-tale hour of midnight but at eleven, when the ball is scheduled to end. That's when we'll have to go back to hiding out.

But until then? Having our first chance to do something in public together as a couple, even if we have to hide behind costumes?

That's magic.

• • •

I wish I could pick up Kat instead of the other way around but that's not how this particular story goes. We have to rely on Kent to drive us. He's the only one who knows what's going on; plus, he's the only one with a driver's license. I'm not sure what Kent thinks of all this, but when he picks me up at the end of the driveway and I climb into the back of the limo, he's perfectly courteous. Climbing in is not as simple as you'd think given the bulk of the Tin Man suit.

Still it's worth it, because there's Kat waiting for me, looking totally adorable in her Toto costume. I mean, I'm not sure she actually looks like Toto, what with all those colored streamers attached to her puffy suit and hood, and that gold makeup all over her face with whiskers drawn on. Maybe she misunderstood and thought I said the Cowardly Lion? But she is adorable.

"Hello, Mr. Kent," I say, on my best behavior. "Thank you for driving us, sir."

"Mr. Kent is my father," Kent says, eyeing me sternly in the rearview mirror. "Just Kent'll do."

"Yes, sir."

"And no 'sir' either."

"Okay . . . Kent."

Still eyeing me in the mirror, he puts the car in gear.

I'd like to tell Kat how great she looks, how excited I am about the night to come, but it's too awkward with her Secret Service agent right up front. I wonder how well he can see the road given how steadily he's eyeing me in that mirror.

So I do the one thing I *can* do. I reach out and take one of Kat's hands, squeezing the fingers beneath her costume furry paw with one of my own hands, covered with silver makeup.

There are cars pulling up to the drop-off lane in front of Will-field Academy, but Kent pulls around to the back of the school. Even if we're in costume, Kat says this particular limousine would be very recognizable to the other kids arriving and we don't want to give the game away.

It's amazing all the little details you have to think of and bases to cover when you're trying to get away with something.

"I'm not sure I should be doing this," Kent says, putting the car in park, "aiding and abetting you two."

"Well, we appreciate it, sir."

"What did I tell you about that? Just don't get into any trouble and be sure to be out here by eleven."

"I'll take good care of her."

He gives me one last glare in the mirror before nodding curtly. "Be sure you do."

And then it's like we're released. As Kent leisurely moves to get out of his seat, I open my door, haul myself out, and hurry around the car so I can get there first to open Kat's door for her. All of which is easier in theory than in practice in a Tin Man costume.

Holding the door, I reach down and grab hold of Kat's outstretched paw to help her out.

"Nice move," Kent observes.

"Thank you."

With one leg back in the car he adds, "Be sure to keep it up."

Before I can offer reassurance on that front, he slams the door, but then opens the window. "Remember what I said," he says. "Be out here by eleven sharp, because I'll be waiting. And if you're not out in time?" He glares at me. "I'm storming the place." The window shuts before I can respond.

Kat laughs. "He's just being overprotective."

"You think?"

"I'm sorry. Did that bother you?"

"No. It's kind of nice to think of someone looking out for your best interests when I'm not around."

And it is. From what Kat has told me, it's not like her dad pays much attention to her interests—not unless it somehow affects one of his campaigns—and she doesn't really remember her mom.

"I'm glad you've got him," I say.

"I'm glad I've got you," she says, slipping her hand into mine.

We walk around to the front of the school to join the line of ticket holders waiting to get in. Even though Kat's in costume, it's tough to take my eyes off her. But when I finally do, I notice something unexpected.

"Um, Kat? Why does everyone else look like they just stepped out of a Shakespeare play or some episode of *Masterpiece* with masks?"

I'm still laughing as we tumble into the gym with the rest of the crowd.

"Weren't you the one who said," I say, laughing so hard it's tough to get the words out, "that Willfield Academy just likes to call things by fancy names and that the masquerade ball was just a fancy name for a regular costume party? Well, look around you, Kat: I'm pretty sure this is a masquerade ball!"

She looks around us.

"Are you sure," I say, "that you didn't get it mixed up with what they do for Halloween?"

People are staring at us like crazy—we look so out of place—and yet, I don't care. I'm with Kat. And anyway, with these costumes, no one can tell who we are.

"I didn't know," Kat says. And that's when I notice the look of dismay on her face, beneath her sparkly gold makeup. "I've never come to one of these things before."

"It's okay, Kat," I say.

"It is? You don't feel ridiculous?"

I shrug and smile. "Of course I feel ridiculous. But so what? No one even knows who we are. And if they did? Still, so what?"

She smiles then.

"You know," I say, "I hate to break this to you, but between the face makeup and the furry thing over your head, you look more like a lion than a dog."

"Oh, great. Well, thanks. You know, it's not easy making your own costume."

"No, it's not. Dance with me?"

"No, thank you."

"Come on." I take her paw and gently tug her toward the floor, where all the dukes and duchesses are gyrating like crazy to some fast song. "It'll be fun."

"I don't know how to dance. I'll look silly."

"Seriously?" I laugh, using my free hand to indicate my Tin Man costume. "You think that dancing is what'll finally make us look silly? You don't think that ship has already sailed?"

"Didn't I just mention that I don't know how to dance?"

She may sound like she's resisting but her feet are slowly following me.

"I'll let you in on a little secret I learned," I whisper, "from back when I was younger and my friends and I used to stand at the sidelines at dances."

"What's that?"

"Everyone's self-conscious, everyone worries that other people will see them looking silly. The truth is, everyone is so worried about how they look themselves that no one is really looking at you."

"Oh."

"Plus, another thing I learned from watching. Guys who dance? They have a greater chance of getting kissed at the end of the night."

Kat throws her head back and laughs and then she starts to move. A part of me would like to say that she's a natural. The truth? She dances even worse than she sings. I mean, she looks positively ridiculous. I imagine we both do. And the few times I look around, when I can tear my eyes away from her, I see that despite what I said about other dancers being too wrapped up in themselves to notice what anyone else is doing, a large percentage of the people around us are staring at us like: Who let these two in?

But so what?

Let ridiculousness reign.

The night progresses.

And we do all the normal school-dance things. Except, you know, our way.

When we get out of breath from all the fast dancing, we hit the refreshments table. Since Kat has trouble grasping a cookie herself—you know, paws for hands—I hold it up to her mouth so she can take bites, popping the last bite into my own mouth just in case I got silver makeup on it and the silver makeup is toxic. I may not be dressed like one of these masquerading dukes all around me but at least I can be as chivalrous as one.

And then, more dancing.

It's not until a slow song finally comes on that I look up at the clock on the wall and see that it's five minutes to eleven.

"Last dance!" the DJ calls.

How did that happen?

I look down at Kat and hold my hands out to her, and she takes them with her paws. Then I pull her close, or as close as I can with the Tin Man costume. This is where I've wanted to be all night. This is the moment I've been waiting for: being out in public with my girl, dancing with her in my arms.

Soon, this moment will end and the clock will strike and we'll have to go back to where we were before: hiding in the shadows.

But right now, this is enough.

It's better than enough. It's fantastic.

When Kent pulls up in front of my house, I think again how I wish things were different and our parents weren't, well, competing against each other on a national scale. If I had my license, not only would I have been able to pick Kat up for the dance, but I'd be dropping her off now too, doing the clichéd thing of walking her to her door.

I can't believe I've turned into a guy who wants to be a cliché. But there you have it.

Things aren't different, though, and that means it's Kat walking me to my door instead. Past the bushes, the house in front of us mostly dark—Mom's on the road campaigning, the twins are no doubt asleep, and my dad is who knows where.

But that's okay, because when we get to the door I do something I've been dying to do all night. I push the hood of her costume back, letting her blond hair tumble free. I put my silver hands in her hair and draw her in close until my lips touch hers.

I've been wanting to do this for so many hours, I don't care who sees me do it.

Okay, I suppose only Kent can see, and hopefully he's looking away, but still.

Because as good as the night has been so far, this moment is even better—her hair in my hands, my lips on hers, Kat kissing me back.

I'm so caught up in the moment that I'm startled when Kat pulls away.

"Did you hear something?" she asks.

I'm so distracted by her I can't hear anything, unless it's the sound of my own racing heart. "Like what?" I say, still distracted, lowering my face toward hers, aching to kiss those lips again.

But she remains stiff in my arms.

"It sounded like *rustle* followed by *snick* and then another *snick*," she says.

I force myself to concentrate, to listen for a moment, but there's nothing there.

"Do you still hear it?"

"No," she says, shrugging before adding what may be the most romantic words I've ever heard in my life, words that tell me that she's the one person in the world who knows *exactly* how I feel right now, "it must have been the pounding of my own heart."

I kiss her again.

I wish this moment could go on forever.

KATIE

"Ugh! This makeup—I don't think my skin can breathe under it!"

I'm back in the limo, being driven away.

"Then it wasn't worth it, Miss Katie?"

"Are you kidding me?" I sigh. When I close my eyes, I can imagine the feel of Drew's lips on mine, his arms around me tight, claiming me as his. "It was *so* worth it."

DREW

Not only have I become a cliché, but I'm a romantic fool of a cliché, because, yes, I walk into the house on cloud nine. There's nothing that can spoil my mood, I think, as I shut the front door behind me. Nothing can spoil this night.

That's when I hear my dad's voice call out from his office: "Drew? Is that you?"

"Yeah," I call back.

I follow the trail of the few lights that have been left on back to my dad's office, finding him in his usual spot: behind his desk with the back of his laptop facing the door.

I wonder how I'm going to explain my strange costume to him, but in the end I don't have to. Because after he looks at me and mutters a "What the . . .?," he stops, his voice catching.

"Dad? What is it?" I ask, fear setting in. Are those tears

in my dad's eyes? I've never seen him cry before. "What's wrong?"

That's when he turns the laptop so that it's now facing me and I can see what he's been looking at.

"Drew," my dad says, "I swear, it's not true."

KATIE

I don't know how I manage to get to sleep, but I do and have only the finest of dreams. And when I wake on Saturday morning? It's to the glorious sound of the phone ringing, followed by Cook yelling up the stairs for me.

I nearly trip over my feet in my effort to race downstairs, skidding to a stop in front of Cook, who's holding the landline out to me.

Landlines—what a wonderful thing.

"It's that boy who calls sometimes," Cook says.

As if I need to be told who it is, I think, smiling inside as I take the phone from her.

"Hello?" I say, so eager to talk to Drew, so eager to hear him say that he had as good a time as I did last night.

But first my greeting is met with a long moment of silence. And then: "How could you do it?" a voice I barely recognize says.

"Excuse me? Drew?"

"Who else would it be? Who else . . . *trusted* you?"

Immediately I'm on the defensive, even though I have no clue what I have to be defensive about. "What are you talking about?"

"The news. Haven't you seen the news yet?"

"No. I just got up." There's a sense of foreboding in my stomach and it just keeps growing. "Why? What's wrong?"

"As if you don't know."

"But I don't! Drew, what is it?"

"It's all over the news. Some 'unidentified source'"—Drew endows these last two words with more venom than I've ever heard two words endowed with— "has told the press that my dad is cheating on my mom."

"That's horrible! What kind of awful person would do such a thing?"

Another moment of silence. And then somehow, even more venom:

"You."

And now I'm horrified on an entirely different level.

"You can't possibly think—"

But I get no further because he again snarls, "I . . . *trusted* you," only now, sickeningly, I know what he means. "You were the only person I told—so who *else* could it be?"

"Someone else, *anyone* else, it just wasn't—"

"I don't want to hear it, *Katie*."

I can't speak. I'm not Kat anymore?

"I trusted you. I believed in you. But all the while you were just setting me up to get info for your dad's campaign. Not using the info right away? That was a move of sheer brilliance. You waited until I fell for you, so you could cause the most damage. Maybe you even thought I'd never guess it was you. But since I told no one else, who could it really be?"

After all the years I've spent helping my father write campaign speeches—after the thousands upon thousands of words I've written in the cause of persuading others to our point of view—in the end, when I open my mouth to defend myself, no words will come.

Then I hear the worst words of all:

"Good-bye, Katie. I never want to see you again."

DREW

I know that was the right thing to do, that I had no other choice.

So why does it hurt so bad?

KATIE

This morning I woke with such clarity of purpose: knowing things were solid between me and Drew, eager to talk to him on the phone because this thing—us, together—has become the best thing in my life.

But now?

It's like I'm moving in a fog, placing the landline on the foyer table, and starting the slow trudge back up the long flight of stairs.

Then I think: Wait a second. I'm a Willfield. Willfields don't take things lying down. Willfields meet challenges head-on!

Maybe, I don't know, Drew's wrong somehow. Maybe he read the story incorrectly. This has to be a mistake. It just has to be.

I race back up the rest of the stairs to my room, turn on my computer, and defy my father's ban: I access the Internet, hoping against hope—like Truman defeating Dewey (even though Truman was a Democrat, it's still a great analogy for this)—that this can all still turn out okay.

Sometimes, like with the 2000 and 2004 elections, there's a long period of suspense in which observers wonder: How will this all play out?

But no sooner do I access the Internet than I see the screaming headlines on page one:

PRESIDENTIAL HOPEFUL NOT WOMAN ENOUGH FOR FIRST HUSBAND WANNABE?

The piece that follows is filled with speculation and innuendo, and none of it looks good, all coming from the old (un)reliable "unconfirmed source."

I ask myself again how Drew can possibly think I was behind this. I know what he said—that I was the only person he told etcetera—but doesn't he know me better by now? Shouldn't he believe me? Shouldn't he believe *in* me?

I'm sad, I'm mad, I'm so many different emotions swirling all at once that I can't even name them all.

I look at the pictures accompanying the piece—of Drew's mother; of his parents together, in happier times; of the whole Reilly family—and it occurs to me that there's something missing. Where in all of this is there a picture of the supposed "other woman"? Shouldn't there be something more here than innuendo and speculation and an "unconfirmed source"?

Apparently though, people don't need any more than that to believe the worst because as I scan through the reader comments and see what a few months ago I would have given all the money in my trust fund to see—the electorate dumping on my father's opponent—I wince at the harsh unfairness and sheer meanness in people's responses.

Most are some version of "I prefer my sex scandals after the election, thank you very much," with the absolute worst being "If Samantha Reilly's own husband doesn't want her then why should we?"

I'm still wincing as I close out the piece when the home page revolves to the second-biggest article of the day and that's when I see it:

REILLY ELDEST SON IN THE LION'S DEN?

Beneath this headline, there is a picture, several of them:

The first is of a Tin Man, pushing back Toto's hood, and the others are all of the Tin Man kissing Toto once the hood has been removed. It's obvious, with my hair free, that Toto is me. And even though Drew's identity is less obvious, what with the silver all over his face, there's no mistaking the fact that we're standing in front of the Reilly home.

I suppose I should be thankful for that "Reilly Eldest Son" part—at least no one is trying to say that I'm the other woman in his father's affair, which would be totally gross—but a part of my mind objects: "*Lion?* Can't they see I'm a dog? I'm supposed to be Toto!"

Apparently though, plenty of people do think I'm a dog, appearance-wise and politically—people on the Internet can be so cruel—because that's pretty much the substance of the first page of comments. I *X* out the screen. I simply cannot stand to look at it anymore.

Who would do such a thing? And where on earth did someone get those pictures?

Then I remember the night before.

Drew kissing me. Me thinking I heard sounds coming from the bushes.

Rustle.

Snick.

Snick.

Someone took pictures of us then? But who? Why?

I remember asking Drew and him saying that he didn't hear anything.

And then it hits me.

What if he was lying? What if he already knew about the story breaking about his father and blamed me for it? Maybe he planted a photographer there? Maybe he just went through with the evening so he could set me up for a big embarrassment in order to get back at me?

Because looking again at that first page of comments, I am nothing if not embarrassed.

I don't know what to think anymore.

I'm starting to move more firmly from sad into angry when I feel a soft brush of fur against my ankles and see Dog down there.

I pick him up and bury my face in his fur.

"How, Dog?" I ask. "How did something that felt so good turn into something that feels so bad?"

DREW

It seems like weeks since I've seen my mom, but this morning she flies home from the campaign trail.

"Family meeting" are the first words out of her mouth when she comes through the door.

"Us too?" Max and Matt ask.

"Just Drew and Dad," she says. She gives them quick hugs before sweeping toward her office, my dad and me in tow.

"Is it true?" she asks my dad as soon as the door is closed.

The last thing I want is to be witness to the breakup of my parents' marriage. Why am I even here?

"No," my dad says. His answer is so instant and direct, for the first time, I don't doubt him. "We may be having our share of problems—a presidential campaign isn't really the best thing for quality time—but I would never do something like this to you, Sam. You have to know that. I would never *want* to do something like this."

It's obvious from my mom's expression that she believes him too. But:

"This couldn't come at a worse time," she says. "Treadwell was gaining in the polls as it was—but now? With *this*?"

"But if it's not true," I say, going on to use political language I didn't even know I possessed, "how can they make it stick?"

My mom snorts. "You try proving a negative. Once the media get an idea into the electorate's collective brain, it doesn't matter much anymore what's true or not. What I'd love to know is . . . where did they even get the idea in the first place?"

I really don't want to do this but: "From me?" I wince out the answer.

"*What*?" My parents may not have been unified in much these past few months but they are most certainly unified in this.

Barely even able to get the words out, I explain. I tell them about Kat— Scratch that. I tell them about how *Katie* and I became friendlier after our joint appearance on *That Morning Show*, her giving me a lift home, me inviting her to come work on the Corvair, and all the rest. And I admit that I was the one who told her about my dad maybe having an affair.

"Why would you say such a thing?" my dad demands.

"Because I thought it was true!" I practically scream back.

"Based on what?"

"You guys have been fighting a lot, you haven't been going on the campaign trail with her as often as you did before, and sometimes if I come in the room and you're talking on the phone, you quickly wrap up the call . . ."

"Drew," my dad says, "I do that because I want to pay attention to you when you're home."

"Which *you* almost never are," I point out.

"I'm an adult. I am allowed to leave the house. And you're always in that garage!"

He has a point there, maybe more than one.

But I persist. "Then why did you hire the nanny, Stella, if you wanted to pay more attention to us?"

"Because there are three of you and only one of me, *and* I also wanted to be available to your mom if she needed me."

"But you've been campaigning with her less."

"You already said that. And if you'd given me a chance to explain—or, better yet, asked me when these things first started bothering you—I would have told you that your mother and I agreed, with Max and Matt still so young, one of us should be here to provide a stabilizing influence."

"But you're not here much," I object.

"Hey, regardless of my work, I sleep under the same roof! If the twins need me at night, they know where to find me!" I see him visibly struggle to rein in his temper before continuing. "As for the fighting, well, married people do that sometimes—it comes with the territory—but it doesn't mean they stop loving each other over every disagreement; perhaps you'll be lucky enough to know that some day. *None* of this adds up to me having an affair."

Oh. *Oh.*

My mom does a surprising thing then: she laughs.

Has she lost her mind? What can possibly be funny in any of this?

"At least," she says, gaining control of herself, "that solves one mystery."

"What?" I say. "That I'm the idiot who told Katie, who in turn told the press? I thought we already established that."

"Well, that too." She pulls out her iPhone, touches some buttons, and then holds out the front of the screen toward me, and that's when I see it:

The picture of me dressed as the Tin Man kissing Katie dressed as Toto outside this very house.

"I was wondering what you were doing," she says, "kissing the enemy."

I am so beyond mortified.

"I didn't know she was like that," I defend myself. "I swear, if I had, I never would have become friends with her in the first place. And I certainly never would have . . ." I wave disgustedly at the phone. "But I've broken up with her. In fact, I'm never going to speak to her again."

"Oh, yes you are."

"What?"

"Not only are you going to speak to her, you're going to continue to date her."

"What?"

Has all the election stress finally gotten to her? Has my mom completely taken leave of her senses?

"You *owe* me this, Drew," she says, a steel in her voice that reminds me how she's gotten as far as she has in the first place. "If it weren't for your girlfriend, I wouldn't be in this mess in the first place. You *owe* me this."

Okay. All right already. I owe her.

But what?

What do I owe her?

KATIE

Early in the afternoon, I hear a commotion coming from the foyer. I go to the top of the stairs and see my father standing there with Marvin. Without thinking, I fly down the stairs and throw myself into my father's arms.

"Hey," he says, "that's some greeting! What's the occasion?"

"I'm just happy to see you," I say, and I am. After everything I've been through, it just feels so good to see a friendly face; to see someone who, no matter what, is always in my corner.

"What are you doing home?" I say. "I thought today you were supposed to be in"—I try to remember which stop was scheduled—"Arkansas?"

"Kansas," he corrects, "but I can see where you'd make that mistake. I get them confused all the time too. Giving two states such similar names—what were the Founding Fathers thinking of?" He's briefly perplexed, obviously giving this some deep consideration, but then shrugs it off. "I thought I'd take a break and come see my favorite girl. Is there something wrong with that?"

"Nothing at all," I say, putting my arm around his waist for a second hug, this one more of a half hug.

"And," he adds, "I wanted to discuss something with you."

"Oh?"

My dad puts one arm around my shoulders and says, "Marvin?" And Marvin trails behind as my father leads us toward his office.

As bad as today has been, I start to feel excited. Perhaps my father wants me to assume a bigger role in the campaign? Something larger than myself to help me take my mind off my problems is just what I need.

Once we're in the office, I disengage myself from my father's arm, suddenly eager to begin.

"What did you want to discuss?" I say. "Did you want me to do your stump speech for you in Arkansas? Or Kansas? Maybe both?"

"I want," he says, smiling, "for you to continue your unholy alliance—that is to say, your relationship—with Drew Reilly."

"What?"

"I must admit, when I first learned of it—when Marvin first showed me that picture of you and . . . *that boy* . . . wearing those costumes and . . . *kissing*— I was rather taken aback. And when Marvin further pointed out that, based on the evidence of the costumes, it was unlikely that this was a spur-of-the-moment thing and might be the end product of a longer relationship, I was seriously put out. My baby, consorting with the enemy?

But then I thought, well, I did ask you to be friendlier in order to get intel . . ."

"It wasn't like—"

"And now I think: What could be better for the campaign than this?"

"What?"

"Well, to be fair, it was Samantha Reilly's idea."

"Samantha Rei—" My head is spinning. "Dad, what are you talking about?"

"Did you not hear me? Samantha Reilly. She called me earlier today."

"What? *Why?*"

"She said that, in light of recent events—falling overnight poll numbers for both of us; her because of the recent scandal concerning her husband, me because the press is claiming I run a dirty campaign; the two of us jointly because Bix Treadwell is doing a bang-up job of persuading voters that combined we're just a couple of mudslinging amoral vipers . . . Where was I?"

"What Samantha Reilly said," Marvin prompts, "in light of recent events."

"Thank you, Marvin. Yes, in light of . . . all those things I just said, Samantha Reilly says that the best thing for both of our campaigns would be for you and Drew to keep on seeing each other . . . publicly."

"That's crazy!"

"Not really. In fact, between this idea and the idea she had to take away you kids' technological devices, I'm beginning to think that that Reilly woman has got a lot more on the ball than I previously thought."

"But even if she's right, that this would be good for both campaigns—which she's not—that's just impossible."

"Why?"

"Because Drew and I broke up." If we were ever really even together, which I doubt now, since how could he turn on me so easily.

"Yes," my father muses, "she did say something to that effect. She said the boy told her. But she failed to mention why. Would you care to elaborate?"

"Because Drew thinks I leaked the story to the press about his father having an affair." I still can't believe Drew thinks that.

"Even better," my father says, "brilliant!"

"What?"

"You lulled him into a false sense of security, then you acquired the intel, which you in turn fed to the press—like I believe I said already, brilliant!"

"But I didn't do that!" I'm not sure which horrifies me more right now: that Drew believes this of me or that my father believes it . . . and thinks it's wonderful. "I *wouldn't* do that!"

"No?" My father shrugs. "Well, I suppose that's neither here nor there. Marvin, tell her the plan and why it's so important."

"It's pretty simple, Katie. You and Drew continue seeing each other, but you do so publicly. We make sure there are lots of pictures. When the public sees you together, they'll think: how cute. More important, they'll think: hey, if the two main candidates' kids can get along this well, then whatever noise this third-party candidate is making about them being so awful must be a load of malarkey. We cut Bix out of the picture and the race is back on between your father and Samantha Reilly, and we all know how that story ends."

Sometimes I wonder why my father pays Marvin so much money. Is this seriously the best he can come up with?

"Even if that was a sound plan," I say, "and I'm not agreeing it is, Drew would never agree to it."

"Ah, but he already has," my father says.

I don't believe this. But: "Fine," I say. "Even if that's true, though, it's still a lousy plan."

"Why?"

"Because people won't go for it. They'll hate the idea of Drew and me as a couple."

"How can you say that? Where do you get your crazy ideas from?"

I confess about going online and seeing the picture of Drew and me with all the rude comments underneath. I'm reluctant to use the word "dog" about myself out loud but I have no problem stating, "People were downright nasty about the picture. Believe me, no one wants to see any more pictures of us together."

"Did you get past the first page of comments?" my father says. "First commenters are notoriously harsh." He snaps his fingers at Marvin. "Show her on your i-thing."

Marvin complies and at first there are the same awful comments I saw before. But with a flick, Marvin scrolls down and I see page after page of praise along the lines of "SOOOO *cute*" and "If only Congress got along so well" and "Kew for President." It takes me a while to figure out that last but I make the effort because it has the most likes by far and that's when it hits me:

KEW—they've shipped our names together! (I know all about shipping names because of Cook's obsession with *General Hospital*. She gets these special soap opera magazines, and fans do that with characters all the time.)

I suppose I should be grateful that at least they didn't ship us into DRAT.

"See?" my father says. "People love you together! Why, you could be bigger than that Bieber boy and that Cyrus girl—are they dating?"

"You're really serious about this," I say.

"As a heart attack!" my father says. "You're always saying you're willing to do what it takes to help the campaign."

I am, but I never thought it would entail being coerced into dating a boy I'm no longer dating, having to pretend in public to want to be with him—how painful and awkward is this going to be?

"When you think about it, it's not really for that long," my father says persuasively. "Marvin, how long until the election?"

"Three weeks from Tuesday."

"See?" My father spreads his arms jovially. "You just need to pull this off for a little over three weeks and then you never have to see or talk to him again."

I take a deep breath. "So, when is this all supposed to start? Immediately?"

"Nah," my father says.

"We wouldn't want it to look staged," Marvin says.

"You can start on Tuesday," my father says.

"In St. Louis," Marvin says, "at the first debate."

DREW

"Wow," Sandy says, "I was beginning to think I'd never see this place again."

It's Sunday afternoon and we're in my garage. I called Sandy earlier to invite him over.

"Oh, come on," I say. "It hasn't been that long. What's it been, just a few weeks?"

"A few weeks during which you kept telling me you were too busy with schoolwork to get together."

"Well, I was busy."

"Yeah, but you were busy with Katie Willfield."

"Oh. You've seen the pictures."

"Dude, the whole world has seen the pictures."

Those pictures—I'd love to get my hands around the neck of the person who took them.

"So how come you didn't tell me about it?" Sandy asks.

How come? Because, much as I love Sandy, he's got a big mouth and we were trying to keep things quiet.

"I guess it just never came up," I say.

"Riiiiiight. So, you still seeing this chick?"

"No," I say and then immediately say, "Yes." Because after all the things I haven't told Sandy, I really can't tell him that Katie and I are now broken up but only pretending to be together for the sakes of our parents' campaigns.

"Which is it," Sandy says, "yes or no?"

"No, I'm not seeing her today—I'm hanging with you today—but yes, I'm still seeing her. As a matter of fact, I'm flying out on Tuesday morning to St. Louis to, um, hang with her at the first presidential debate." Before he can press me further, I say, "So, you want to help me figure out how to rebuild this engine?"

KATIE

In all my years of schooling, Monday will no doubt go down in history as the strangest of all.

Since my failed attempts to secure friendships years before, I haven't bothered trying very hard to make friends with kids my own age. But if there is one thing I've learned in my time with Drew, it's that it's nice to have a friend.

So I do something—make that a whole bunch of some-things—that I've never done. I take the time to talk to other people. I compliment them on things they're wearing that I like or on doing well at something in class. Previously self-sufficient, I ask people for help with things. In short, I take an interest. At first, it's just to achieve an end. But as the day goes on, I find myself doing it for the simple pleasure of the thing itself. At first, people are hesitant, kind of like a bunch of Robert De Niros—"Are you talking to me?"—but people are more forgiving than you'd think they'd be. Most people, I think, are always willing to start fresh.

Okay, so maybe it's just one day. And tomorrow I leave for St. Louis and three weeks on the campaign trail. And then there's no telling what will happen after that.

But at least it's a beginning. Who knows? Maybe after all this is over, I'll finally have a life.

DREW

I'm wearing a navy blue suit, white shirt, and navy tie because Ann says that this isn't like the night my mom received the nomination and if I don't dress properly, it'll reflect badly on my mom. The suit has to be navy, Ann told me, because Democrats always wear blue at these events while Republicans always wear red—well, the men don't wear red suits, obviously, but they do wear red ties. If you ask me, this is one of the stupidest things I've ever heard. Like, how stupid do politicians think the American voter really is? Do they honestly think the color of a tie or suit is actually going to make some kind of difference? Like, if the politicians didn't wear the team colors, voters wouldn't be able to tell them apart and would wind up voting for the wrong candidate? Which begs the question: Since Bix Treadwell is the third-party candidate, what team color will he be wearing?

Oh, and my hair? It's trimmed a smidgen and slicked back—more of Ann's ideas.

Yes, that's right, folks. We are live backstage at the first presidential debate. We've got our own room—I can only presume the other candidates' families also have their own rooms—and my dad and I are watching the action on a little TV. The twins are at home with Stella. When the debate is over, Dad and I are supposed to join my mom onstage and that's when the real fun is scheduled to start. Yeah, right. After congratulating my mom, I'm supposed to hold Katie's hand. This'll be the first time I've seen her since I broke up with her and I'm supposed to act all lovey-dovey. That's the opposite of what I'm feeling for her.

I don't want to think about that right now.

What I'd really like to do is take out my iPhone and distract myself. My mom gave it back to me right before we got here. When I expressed my surprise, she said, "Of course I'm giving it back to you. How else are you going to take selfies of you and Katie when you go out on your date tomorrow?"

Right. My *date*. Tomorrow morning, before leaving town, Katie and I are supposed to go do something in St. Louis and take pictures of ourselves having fun together.

I'm not sure what I'm looking forward to less: holding her hand onstage tonight or going on a date with her tomorrow.

Yes, I would very much like to distract myself from all this by texting Sandy right now. There's just one problem. After giving me my iPhone back with instructions for tomorrow, my mom was quick to warn, "But no getting in trouble." And me and Sandy texting? Given the mood I'm in? That's *bound* to lead to trouble.

Sheesh. I finally get my iPhone back and I'm so scared of doing the wrong thing with it that I can't bring myself to *do* anything with it. What a world.

"I don't believe this," my dad says.

"What?"

"Aren't you watching?" He points at the TV monitor. "That bozo just asked your mom if it ever made her feel guilty, leaving the twins at home while pursuing a life in politics. 'Don't you ever feel torn between your career and your family?'" My dad is clearly outraged on her behalf. "What century are we living in? They don't ask the men those kinds of questions!"

This draws me in a bit to the debate. And the absence of anything else to do in the room draws me in even more. Before I know it, I'm actually watching. Soon, I notice there is a difference in the tenor of the questions addressed to my mom. If it were me, some of those questions might make me mad.

But if my mom's mad, she doesn't show it. In fact, she impresses me with her ability to listen closely to each question, and however ridiculous it might be, answer coolly and calmly. I don't think I could ever do that. For the first time it hits me: she's actually very good at this thing.

And you know who else is good? Edward Willfield. His approach is different than my mom's. While her approach is more serious, his is more one hand in the pocket and a smile, like a favorite uncle casually telling you a story. As I pay more attention, I come to realize that he's very good at not answering the question directly. Instead, he makes it seem like he does but then takes his response time as an opportunity to talk about whatever he wants to. Slick. I may have to try that in Social Studies class sometime—"Your question about the American Revolution is most excellent, Ms. Tomlinson. Now, let me tell you about the Civil War . . ."

You know who isn't good at this debate stuff?

Bix Treadwell.

Not only does he fail to employ Edward Willfield's slick trick of twisting questions to his own purpose, but his answers don't even come close to making any kind of sense! He keeps rambling on about chickens and pots and some bizarre tax scheme that even I can tell would never work. On top of that, every time he's asked a question, he prefaces his response by saying, "If my two esteemed colleagues would just stop slinging mud at each other for a minute so I can talk . . ."

But here's the thing. My mom and Edward Willfield *aren't* slinging mud at each other. They're being so polite, it's like two cartoon characters who want to go through the same doorway— "After you"; "No, I insist, after you"; "No, really"—only to get stuck together in the doorway when they try to pass through at the same time. If they were any more polite, you'd think they were friends. And when they talk, their policies are so close together, it's tough to tell them apart.

Bix Treadwell, though? He makes no sense. Who let this guy in? Oh, right. The voters did, because he's a self-made billionaire who can afford to finance his own election. Which, I suppose, also technically describes my mom.

But still, the guy's a loon!

The least loony person, though?

My mom, by a landslide.

The final question to all three candidates is the same:

"Why do you want to be president?"

Edward Willfield looks taken aback by it, like he wasn't expecting so basic a question. Almost like he prepared for all the tough stuff, and in the process, neglected to consider this. For the first time all night, he falters. His response is scattered and seems to lack focus. Bix Treadwell's response makes absolutely no sense whatsoever.

But my mom's?

"There are only two reasons to run for the highest office in the land," she says, "and they both must be true at the same time. You must believe that things could be better and you must also believe that you're the best person to make it so."

Simple. Direct.

For the first time I think: I'd vote for her!

For the first time I think: She deserves to win.

But then, just like that, it's over. The audience is clapping loudly—during the actual debate they'd been instructed not to, so I guess now they're making up for lost time—and my dad and I are being given the cue to join my mom onstage, which we do.

My dad kisses her, I kiss her. Then, as instructed, we cross the stage to Bix Treadwell's family and congratulate them, do the handshake thing. (For the record, his team color is yellow. I realize it's the only primary color left after red and blue. But if you ask me? It's a mistake.) Finally, after the Willfields have also congratulated the Treadwells, the Reillys and Willfields meet in the middle.

My mom, Dad, and I all congratulate Edward Willfield. Then my mom and dad both shake Katie's hand, and tell her what a pleasure it is to finally meet her. My mom even compliments Katie on her red suit.

And now it's my turn to take Katie's hand and kiss her on the cheek, that cheek that is still *so* soft. The crowd roars the loudest it has all night as I raise our clasped hands in the air.

"Kew! Kew! Kew!" people shout from all over the arena.

If I tried to smile any wider, my face would probably crack. And when I look out of the edge of my eye at Katie, I see that her smile is equally wide and forced.

I can't help myself.

Out of the corner of my mouth, I whisper: "Traitor."

And almost immediately, she whispers right back: "*Jerk.*"

Wait a second.

How am I the jerk here?

KATIE

"So," Kent says brightly from the front seat, "who's up for Cronuts?"

I'm in the back, as far to the right on the seat as I can possibly be, while Drew is as far to the left as he can be. The ocean of empty space between us is huge. Even though I brought several red suits with me—yeah, yeah, I know, they make people think of Christmas when I wear them, but that's what Republicans wear at debates—today I have on the jeans I bought the first time Drew invited me over. I'm also wearing a thick sweater because we're supposed to look like a normal couple in the pictures. Drew has on jeans and a T-shirt. I have a feeling he may regret this in the chilly Missouri weather.

And Kent with his bright offer of Cronuts?

Kent's the only one who knows the real story of everything that's happened with Drew and me. He knows how much I'm hurting. But he's also a romantic and he thinks the situation can still be repaired. That it's all some misunderstanding and we'll laugh about it in the end.

I'm not laughing.

"No Cronuts," I say.

"You sure?" Kent says. "Because—"

"Just drive," I say. "Let's get this thing over with."

It's been decided in advance, by our parents—talk about your unholy alliances!—that we should take pictures of our fake date at the Gateway Arch. It's St. Louis's most significant, recognizable landmark and it has been deemed that this will be the most romantic spot for us.

As we pull up, Drew cranes his head against the window. "Wow, it's big."

I say nothing.

"So tell me," he says. "How did I wind up being the jerk here?"

I snort.

"Well," he says, "that's mature."

"Those pictures?" I say. As if he doesn't already know. "Of us outside your house?"

"How is that my fault?"

"You set me up."

"What?"

I remind him about that night, me saying I heard something—*rustle, snick,* and *snick*—and him saying he didn't.

"You planned it in advance," I say.

"And why would I do that?"

"To embarrass me. You must have known about the story about your dad, you blamed me for that—*which I didn't do*—and you wanted to get back at me."

"What are you talking about? I didn't do that! I *wouldn't* do that!"

"Really?" I stare at him, stony. "Gee, that's what I told you when you accused me. Tell me: How did that work out for me?"

Drew opens his mouth but then closes it, his lips tight together. I've never been the best at reading people, but if I had to guess I'd say he's frustrated.

"You know what?" he says, not waiting for an answer. "Never mind. Let's just do this thing."

He pushes open the door. As he gets out, he's hit with a big gust of wind.

I get out on my side and walk around the back to his. Once there, I see him rubbing his bare arms with his hands.

"Didn't you bring a jacket?" I say. "A sweater?"

"No." He rubs some more, shivers some more.

"St. Louis can get very windy," I say, "and it can be pretty cold already in October."

"Yeah, I noticed."

"Didn't you look at the weather report before coming here? Not to mention, the forecasters say it's going to be an unusually cold fall, especially back home."

"Thank you, *Farmer's Almanac*."

"Funny you should mention that. They say it's supposed to snow as early as the first week in November. I hope it doesn't interfere with voters getting to the polls."

"Not everyone's lives revolve around this stupid election, Katie. I'll be glad when the next three weeks are over with."

"Why? Because we won't have to wonder who the winner is anymore?" I ask. Then I amend with, "Well, unless what happened in 2000 and 2004 happens again." I shudder at the thought.

"No," he says, stopping his rubbing long enough to wave a disgusted hand. "So we don't have to do this. So we don't have to pretend anymore. So we don't have to pretend to like each other."

As if on cue a couple of strangers pass us, smiling. There's something about those smiles. They're not looking at us like, Oh, cute, a couple! They're looking at us more like, Hey, it's them!

Immediately, Drew puts his arm around my shoulders, I put an arm around his waist, we smile at the strangers and then look each other in the eye like there's no place in the world we'd rather be.

After a few moments of this, I say through my forced smile, "Are they gone yet?"

Drew, through his forced smile, responds, "I think so." Then we look all around. The coast clear, we drop our arms and our smiles.

"So," I say, looking at the Gateway Arch. "Should we go up?"

"No. I don't like heights."

"How did I not know that?" I shrug. "I guess it never came up before when we were hanging out in the garage."

At my mention of the garage, I grow wistful and I see a similar look cross Drew's face. Can he be feeling what I'm feeling? *Impossible.* I push the feeling of wistfulness away.

"Well," I say, "if you don't want to go up, would you like to hear about how the Gateway Arch came into existence? Because I was reading up—"

"I don't want an architectural history lesson either." He rubs his arms. "Let's just take the pictures and go."

So that's what we do.

We stand in front of one side of the Gateway Arch, each with one arm around the other, each holding an iPhone out with our other hand, smiling for the unseen public and taking selfies. Then we post them to our various social media handles and send them to a few media sites.

Drew starts to walk away, back toward the limo, but I stay where I am.

He turns back. "What are you doing?"

"I'm waiting," I say.

"For what?"

"For the first comments, to see what people will say."

Even though he must be freezing by now, he comes back and looks at my iPhone with me. I'm feeling nervous because what if they're as mean as those first-page comments were about the masquerade ball pictures?

But they're not.

"Wow," I say in wonder, "they really like us."

No, really, they do. Almost instantly, the first picture has a hundred likes and growing fast.

Drew reads the first few comments out loud. "Kew!" "Kew!" "Kew!"

I laugh. "The first time I heard that out loud, at the debate, all I could think of was Tina Fey's old imitation of Sarah Palin."

I look at Drew, expecting him to find it funny too, but he's just staring at me.

"You know?" I say. I hold my forefingers up like tiny pretend pistols and go, "Pew! Pew! Pew!"

"Never seen it," Drew says, smiling. Only it's a mixed smile, equal parts amusement and appreciation and something else. Sad, maybe.

"Oh, well."

I look back at the screen.

"Oh my goodness," I say. "Did you see this one? 'Just like Romeo and Juliet!' Right. If Romeo and Juliet's families' main bones of contention were how big the defense budget should be and how to improve the tax code."

"Well," Drew says, "hopefully here no one dies in the end."

We both laugh. And we laugh even more as further comments come in. Despite my thick sweater, the wind is strong and I shiver. Almost instantly, I feel Drew's arm go around my shoulders. And without thinking about it first, I rub his bare arm with my free hand.

These actions—his and mine—startle both of us, I think. I can't know what's going on in his head but I certainly know what's going on in mine.

What are we doing here?

I don't know what that commenter who compared us to Romeo and Juliet was thinking. We are nothing like them.

And it has nothing to do with no one dying in the end.

Romeo and Juliet were in love.

We've each hurt each other too much for that.

In wordless agreement, we disengage, put our phones away, head back to the limo.

We drive back in silence to Drew's hotel. He only speaks to me when he gets out, right before he shuts the door:

"See you in Philly."

DREW

The original plan was for me to fly home to Connecticut for most of the week, so I can continue with school until the next debate. But since Katie is spending the entire next three weeks on the campaign trail with her dad, the decision is made that I should do the same with my mom.

"There's no point in letting the opposition get an advantage on us," my mom says. "Plus, sometimes we can learn something from them."

So while my dad flies home every few days to spend some time with the twins, I'm with my mom every step of the way. In the week following the St. Louis debate, we crisscross the country, stopping in a different key state each day.

Wisconsin. South Carolina. Ohio. Michigan. Nevada.

You get the message. There are a lot of states out there.

In the beginning, it's exciting: all that travel on planes, all those states I've never been to before.

It is something of a revelation, being at my mom's side as she gives her speeches, seeing how the people respond to her.

And the questions people—not reporters or TV interviewers, but actual citizens—have for her are an even further revelation. They ask them seriously, clearly concerned about issues I don't normally pay a great deal of attention to, then wait intently to hear what she'll say in return.

What will she do about unemployment?

What kind of plan does she have for improving education?

If Russia does X or North Korea does Y, how will she, as president, respond?

It hits me at some point that it's just a tip of the national iceberg. If we see thousands, even tens upon tens of thousands of people in that first week, they are just a small percentage of the people out there—nameless and faceless people who will never get a chance to ask their questions. There are three hundred million people in the country and it occurs to me that each one of them has questions and concerns. Each one of them has things they'd like to see become better in this country and they're hopeful one of the candidates can make the improvements they seek come to pass.

My mom clearly hopes that person will be her.

Sometimes in conversation I find it tough to maintain one hundred percent focus. When I was still with Katie, I could do that. But you know how it is. Lots of times, people are talking to you and what you're mostly focusing on isn't what they're saying, so that you can respond to it fully, but rather on what you want to say next. Or you're thinking of what you're going to do next or even: Hey, what's for lunch? But my mom, no matter how many times she's heard a question before or how rambling the questioner's delivery, maintains a constant laser-like focus that is nothing short of impressive.

She is even more impressive when faced with the same rude question at each campaign stop.

No matter how people might try to dress it up, no matter how they might try to make it sound like a new question, it always boils down to this: "Is it true that your husband is cheating on you?"

The first time I heard someone ask her that to her face—which is so different, so much ruder than seeing the words in print—I wanted to leap into the crowd and punch the person in the nose. And from the brief tightening in my mom's jaw—so brief, if you blinked you would miss it—I got the distinct impression that she would have liked to do some punching too. But what did she do?

She *smiled.*

And then she said: "Yes, I've read those unconfirmed reports in the press too. And I suppose I'd be troubled by them, as you so clearly are, if they were anything more than unconfirmed. But the truth is, they're not. What is confirmed is that people like you—and everyone here today, everyone across the country—have legitimate concerns about the current state and future of this great country of ours. So what do you say we forget about gossip and instead focus on working together to make these United States the best they can be?"

She gets a roar of approval each time she says this, and each time I feel a surge of pride.

She is, quite simply, that good.

But there's no getting around the fact that the story does persist in the media, which just won't let it go.

"But Dad said it wasn't true," I object.

"I know, and I believe him," my mom says. "Just ignore it."

"It isn't fair, though!"

"You can't worry about 'fair' in politics. Once a story has made front-page news it's almost impossible to get a retraction. And even if you do get one, it's likely to be buried so far back that no one sees it. Or if they do, years later, all people remember is the accusation, not the result."

"So what can we do?"

"About the rumor?"

I nod.

"Nothing." She shrugs. "All we can do is what we've been doing all along: answer people's questions, address their concerns, keep fine-tuning our plan to make tomorrow a better day."

It's late Monday night when we have this talk. Early tomorrow morning, we're supposed to fly into Philadelphia for the second of the three debates. There's now just fifteen days left until Election Day, just a third of the way through this imposed stint of me being on the road.

I know I said it was exciting flying from state to state. And it was. At first. But just one week in, I'm already feeling the fatigue. And if I'm feeling this way after such a relatively short period of time, what must my mom be feeling? After all, she's been living this life on the road for over a year now, first campaigning for the party nomination and now for the national one.

Not to mention, it's kind of lonely on the road. Sure, it's cool seeing my mom in action and it's even sort of interesting to hear her strategy sessions late at night with Ann and other people. And when my dad is with us, I can see that there's still a lot of good between them. But it's still lonely. I never thought I'd say this about that huge house we live in now, but I miss my home. I miss Sandy. I even miss the twins. Mostly, I just miss *normal*.

I can't believe I'm saying this either, but a part of me is actually looking forward to Philly tomorrow and seeing Katie again. At least she's someone I know, someone who isn't Ann or one of the legion of adults surrounding my mom. She's someone I could laugh with. Someone I do laugh with.

Of course I push *that* thought away, almost as immediately as it entered my mind. What am I thinking? The girl's a traitor.

"You okay, bud?" my mom says, covering my hand with hers.

"I'm fine," I say.

"You sure?"

I can't tell her what I've just been thinking so I resort to the truthful things: "Sometimes I just miss home a bit, and Sandy, but it's all fine."

Late at night like this, with the crowds behind us for the time being and her makeup off, I can see how tired she is as she sympathetically pats my hand.

"You really want this thing," I say, "don't you?"

Without me having to define it, she knows exactly what "this thing" is.

"Yes," she says. "After your dad and you kids, it's the thing I've wanted most in my life."

"I hope you get it, then," I say, meaning it. "I think you'd be great."

KATIE

Life on the campaign trail after all these years still fits me like a glove. Flying into a new state each day really helps if you already have your own private jet. Breakfast with one group of voters, speech, speech, lunch in a local spot, speech, speech, dinner with major investors, speech, check the poll numbers, panic, adjust the speeches for the next day accordingly, and then grab a few hours' sleep. Wash, rinse, repeat. And through it all?

Smile, smile, *smile*!

"Do I look okay, baby?" my father asks.

We're backstage in Philly and he's waiting to go on.

"You look fine," I say, adjusting his tie. "You're going to do great. Just remember: No looking at your watch, no sighing, and no matter how infuriating you might find the other candidates' comments or the host's questions, no talking over other people's words. Polls show that voters really frown on all those things."

"You've always got my back, don't you?"

"As long as I'm breathing."

Despite my father's concerns, the Philly debate goes as well as the St. Louis debate did. If I'm being honest, Drew's mother does well too. Really, it's just Bix Treadwell who comes across as being from some completely other planet.

The only awkward moment in the evening comes when the candidates' families go onstage to do the whole congratulations/handshake/kiss/smile thing, and Drew and I meet in the middle to join hands.

Progress has been made. This time, there's no "traitor" or "jerk."

But you know, it's still in the air.

"You know what I was thinking, baby?" my father asks.

We're back at the hotel and he's loosened his tie.

"What's that?"

"Maybe more is more."

"I'm not following. I thought less was supposed to be more."

"Usually, that's true. But this past week we've been doing just a bit better in the polls. And while I'd like to attribute that solely to my own charms, perhaps part of the reason is due to you and Drew?"

I narrow my eyes at him. "What exactly are you saying?"

"If people went gaga, and they did, over those photos of you and Drew last week—and that was just a few measly pics snapped at the Gateway Arch—just think of how much more excited they'd be to have even more."

Which is how I wind up with a directive to spend not just a little time before jetting off to the next stop, but a whole half day tomorrow.

With Drew.

I plan the itinerary carefully in advance to maximize the time, so voters can see pics of us in popular settings, the kinds of places two fun-loving teens might visit together if they were really in love.

We make a brief visit to Longwood Gardens. So romantic. Could anything be more amazing than the Silver Garden? Maybe there *are* more romantic places to get married than the White House. After taking a handful of selfies of us standing with our arms around each other in the Orchid House, which we post to Instagram—Kew! Kew! Kew!—we head to Citizens Bank Park, home of the Philadelphia Phillies. All the while, despite Kent's encouragements from up front, there's not a whole lot of talking involved outside of Where do you think we should stand? and Do you think it looks more authentic if I hug you like this or like this?

At Citizens Bank Park we're allowed out on the field because, hey, VIP treatment!

Someone from the stadium gives us some bats and some balls, and for the first time, Drew looks excited.

"You want me to, um, throw some to you so you can hit them?" I offer.

Drew picks up a bat, but it turns out that, after repeated effort, I can't get the ball over the plate. So Drew just throws some balls in the air for himself, and hits them as they drop down in his field of vision.

That sound of the bat striking the ball—*crack*—is very satisfying.

"That looks like fun," I finally say. "You're pretty good at that."

"Here." He holds the bat out to me. "Do you want to try?"

I hesitate.

"Come on," Drew says. "I'll pitch them to you slow and easy."

I decide to go for it. I mean, really, when else am I going to get an opportunity to bat in a deserted major-league stadium, with no one there to laugh at me when I fail?

But of course, as soon as I take a position beside the plate, bat resting on my shoulder, Drew starts to laugh at me from halfway to the mound.

"What's so funny?" I call out.

"That's not how you hold a bat."

"It's not?"

"No, it's definitely not."

"But that's how you did it."

More laughter. "I can assure you, Katie, that whatever I was doing, it wasn't that thing you're doing right there."

Hey, now.

"You need to choke up on the bat more," he directs me, putting one fist on top of the other.

I squint back at him. "I need to what?"

"Here." Drew walks in my direction. "Let me show you."

Before I know what's happening, he walks over and positions himself behind me, hands over mine, moving them up the bat until they're in the position he thinks they should be. I feel the warmth of his hands and feel his chest against my back. The softness of his breath on my neck from behind makes me shiver.

"Hey," I say, laughing nervously. "Don't get any ideas back there."

"No ideas." One hand leaves mine—I ache for it to return as soon as it's gone—and a moment later there's an iPhone staring me in the face. Drew's snapped our picture.

"There," he says. "I just wanted to make sure it would look right—you know, for the audience. We wouldn't want people to start thinking these pictures were all staged, that they're not authentic or something."

Yeah. Too bad I loved every second of it.

And then, already, it's time for the last stop of the half-day's itinerary: lunch.

"I was thinking," I say in the limo, after reviewing my notes, "Pat's King of Steaks for Philly cheese steak sandwiches? The steak sandwich was invented at Pat's in 1930. Some people say it was Geno's Steaks that added the cheese in 1966. But I'm thinking we go with Pat's. Or better yet, go to *both* places, so that voters can't accuse us of having favorites and we will have covered all our cheese-steak bases?"

Drew just laughs.

"What?" I say, looking up.

"You sure do a lot of research on this stuff."

"Oh, yeah? Well, if you'd done any research back in St. Louis, you wouldn't have wound up freezing in that T-shirt at the Gateway Arch."

"You know," I can't help but inform Drew as we enter Pat's King of Steaks, "this place is open seven days a week, twenty-four hours a day."

"Imagine that? Well, good thing we're not going to be here that long. Maybe we should just order and get this over with?"

How rude.

Still, as we wait in line, once again, I can't stop myself. I lean into Drew, whisper, "I read that they prefer for you to order as quickly as possible. So, like, say, if you want one cheese steak with cheese and fried onions? You say 'one whiz with.'"

He just stares back at me.

"The 'whiz,'" I explain in a further whisper, "stands for Cheez Whiz."

More staring.

"Or, you know, you could have it with another kind of cheese, only then you wouldn't say 'whiz.' Instead, you'd say provolone or whatever cheese you do want."

More staring.

"But really, the most authentic way is to have it with whiz. Of course you can also say 'one whiz without,' if you don't like fried onions, but really, the most authentic thing is—"

He puts both hands out and makes a simmer-down motion. "Thank you, Ms. Travel Brochure, I think I've got it now."

And ouch again.

Still, it's somewhat gratifying to hear him order "Two whiz with" when it's our turn in line. "You wanted one too, right?" he says, turning to me. It's even more gratifying, once we have our grinders and drinks, to sit down in a booth and open my mouth wide and take a big chunk out of the soft roll, thin steak, fried onions, and gooey processed cheese.

"Oh my gosh," I say, not even caring that I haven't entirely swallowed everything in my mouth yet, "this is just *so good*."

The nice thing about food is that, if you're hungry enough and what's in front of you is yummy, you don't have to worry about making conversation. You can just put aside the awkwardness you feel when you're with the other person who's across the table from you and give in to the mouth-feel joy of the moment.

But that moment passes all too quickly.

I wad up my napkin, toss it on the table.

"You know," I say, "I could go for another of these."

"Are you serious?" Drew stares at me.

"Well," I admit, "I was only half kidding before when I suggested going to Geno's too so we could be sure to court one hundred percent of the cheese-steak-eating voters. But now? I could definitely eat another." I point at his empty plate and challenge, "Couldn't you?"

Before you know it, we're laughing our way across the street, laughing our way through ordering another round of "Two whiz with!"

Sitting down with our fresh sandwiches, we each take healthy bites.

"So," Drew says, "which do you think is better?"

"I'm not saying."

"Because you're scared of offending half the voters?"

"No, because they're both so good, I simply don't care." I laugh and take another huge bite, realizing there is a string of cheese still outside my mouth. I try to wipe it away, miss, and decide I don't care.

"I love that about you," Drew says, laughing too.

Only now I'm not laughing too. "What did you just say?"

Now he's not either. "Nothing."

"No, you just most definitely said something."

"It's just that . . ."

"It's just that what?"

"When you're like this . . . so open and laughing at stupid stuff . . ." He gestures at me impatiently. "It's tough to believe that *this* is the same person who betrayed me."

That, like so much else today, stings.

"You know what they say the sign of an intelligent person is?" I ask.

"I suppose you're going to tell me?"

"It's the ability to hold two seemingly conflicting thoughts in your mind at once. So you should be able to think, Wow, I'm upset about what she did, and Wow, she's funny and she's cute when she's eating cheese steak, all at the same time without having your head explode. People are more than just one thing. Most people, Drew, are pretty complex."

He opens his mouth and then shuts it again.

"Also," I say, "it should make it easier for you to keep your head from exploding, since I never did anything wrong in the first place."

Again, he opens his mouth. Again, he shuts it.

I decide that I don't care what he has to say or has decided not to say as I take another healthy bite.

I am *not* going to let him spoil this cheese steak for me.

DREW

We're waiting backstage in Tucson for the start of the third and final debate when it occurs to me that someone's missing.

"Where's Dad?" I say. "He should be here."

He really should. My mom has been doing better in the polls lately, but if my dad's not here for this, tongues are sure to start wagging again. That's all we need.

"Don't worry," my mom says. "He'll be here."

And, true to her word—his too, I suppose—he is. At zero hour, he walks in with the twins and Clint. I guess they figure that, with it being the last debate and all, it's more important to have a solid show of family unity than worry about the twins missing school.

We're all hugging and greeting each other when Dad says to me, "Oh, and I have a surprise for you." He goes to the door, says something to someone out in the hall, and a minute later there's a familiar face standing in the doorway.

"Sandy!" I practically scream.

"Dude." He's wearing jeans and a T-shirt as he ambles over. When he reaches me, we do the guy hug thing.

"What are you doing here?" I say when we disengage.

"Your mom's idea." He gives a nod at her. "Hey, Mrs. Reilly."

"Sandy." She nods back before turning to me. "You've been so good about helping me with the campaign. And you told me how much you missed Sandy. So I thought I'd fly him out. Maybe tomorrow, you could spend the whole day with Katie, and Sandy could go too?"

"Yeah," Sandy says, "how are things going with your . . . *girlfriend*?"

The word brings me up short and I have to remind myself what Sandy knows and what he doesn't. He didn't know I was seeing Katie in the first place. But then, when the rest of the world found out about us because of that photo—which Katie believes I leaked—he found out too. Then, I would have told him the truth, that Katie and I had broken up—well, I broke up with her—but my mom came up with her scheme for us to pretend-date in order to help the campaign and I decided it wouldn't be safe to tell Sandy that.

Yeah, I think that's everything.

"It's fine," I tell Sandy now. "Everything is going great."

"That's terrific." Sandy opens his arms wide. "And who better to play the chaperone?"

Something about the way he says it makes me think: Did my mom really ask him here out of the goodness of her heart, for me, or is this just something she thinks will be good for the campaign?

In the end, I decide it doesn't matter. Whatever the case, I'm just glad he's here.

Then Ann tells my mom it's time, and off she goes.

We stay in the backstage room, watching the debate on the monitor. I've seen two of these already, so you'd think it would be old hat by now, even boring. But the truth is, the suspense has been ratcheted up—it's astounding to believe the election is just one week from today. Even the twins are silent, all eyes glued to Mom every time she speaks.

"She's so good." Sandy breaks the silence.

She is, isn't she? I think.

Still, it's hard not to feel insecurity creeping in.

"Do you really think so?" I ask. Because the truth is, it's impossible to tell what the live audience thinks. They're not supposed to clap or give any indication of support during the actual debate. So even though *I* think she's good, who knows how it's playing to everyone else?

"Totally," Sandy says. "She's got this thing."

I hope he's right. But again, who knows?

Because if there's one thing I'm learning, it's that the American voter is a very fickle beast.

And then, before I know it the final debate is over and it's time for the family to go out on the stage and make all happy-smiley. It's time for me to once again make it look like Katie and I are one ecstatic couple.

In the doorway, I turn back to Sandy.

"You coming?"

"*Dude.* I may be family, but I'm not *that much* family. Besides, look at me." He indicates his T-shirt and jeans. "I'll just watch the festivities on the monitor."

After the festivities, as Sandy put it, and during the limo ride back, Sandy remains uncharacteristically quiet. But once we're back at the hotel and we're safely in our room, he turns on me.

"So," he says. "You want to tell me what's really going on?"

"What do you mean?"

"You and your 'girlfriend.'"

He does the air-quotes thing, which is still so annoying.

"I don't know what you're talking about," I say.

"Come on. I've got two eyes. Maybe other people might be fooled but I'm not."

"Still don't know what you're talking about," I say, chucking a pillow at him. "Hey, you want something from this minibar? I mean, we can't take any of the little booze bottles—they count everything—but how about a soda?" I pull a canister of something out of the fridge, shake it so it rattles. "Cheese curl?"

"I do not want a cheese curl, Drew." And now, having said that, there's no stopping him. "You and that chick—you're not really a couple anymore, are you?"

"I don't know what you're talking about." Suddenly, this is all I can think of to say, my answer to everything. And back to the minibar. I wave a candy bar at him. "Toblerone?"

He doesn't even bother to respond to my offer of food products this time.

"The two of you," he says, "you were holding hands and everything, everything *looked good*, but you didn't say a single word to one another, and the way you had those tight smiles, the way you kind of glared at each other out of the corners of your eyes . . ."

"What did you expect us to say? With the whole world watching? Ooh, ooh, I love you?"

"No, of course not, but I expected *something*. Instead, it seemed to me like it was just for show. So I ask you again: You're not a couple anymore, are you?"

He's asking me? Sounds to me more like he's telling me.

I feel myself wavering.

"Come on, Drew," he says. "I'm your best friend. You can tell me anything."

I've been keeping secrets about this from Sandy for so long, it's become a habit. But his words remind me: no matter what my reservations, he *is* my best friend, always has been. I don't know if it's the late hour or the long days or just because it's such a relief to finally be talking to a real friend after the past lonely weeks on the campaign trail, but I find myself telling him the truth. I tell him everything.

"Wait a second," he says at one point. "Back up. *Katie* was the one who told the press that story about your dad having an affair?"

I shrug. "Who else could it be? She's the only one I ever told."

We both wince. Neither of us say out loud that I clearly didn't trust him.

"So then I broke up with her," I say. "I mean, of course I did."

"But how could you be sure it was her?"

"How could I be sure it wasn't?"

"Did she confess?"

"Well, no. She said it wasn't her. But of course she'd say that, wouldn't she?"

"If she said she didn't, though, and you really liked her, why didn't you just trust her?"

The way he says it now, I start to wonder: Why didn't I?

"Maybe you were wrong," he says.

Could I have been . . . wrong?

"Maybe you should try to make things right with her," Sandy says.

"But she's the one—"

"You don't know that!" he cuts me off.

"Okay," I say. "Let's say you're right. Let's say it wasn't her who told the press. Even if that's the case, she'd never go back out with me now."

"How come?"

So I explain about the pictures from outside my house after the masquerade ball. I explain how Katie thinks it was something I staged to humiliate her.

"Oh." An odd expression comes over Sandy's face. "Dude," he says, "I took those pictures."

"You're kidding, right?" I laugh nervously. "Why would you do such a thing?"

"Jealousy." He says it so simply that I instantly know it's true.

"But why? How? What did you have to be jealous of?"

"You weren't telling me anything. For the first time since I've known you, you were unavailable. I'd call and you'd say you were busy doing homework or something—I knew it couldn't be that. So then I started occasionally stopping by your house, you know, to see if I could find out anything. It wasn't stalking but it just made me crazy, not knowing. That one night, when you were all dressed up as the Tin Man, I got lucky. But then I couldn't believe who the girl you were with was."

"That it was Katie?"

"Yes, *Katie*, the girl you were obsessed with when we were kids."

"Obsessed with . . ." Huh? "*What* are you talking about?"

"Come on, Drew, you know."

"No, I really don't."

"When we were four, we met her at that outdoor festival at the end of the summer. Her dad was campaigning there and you two, I don't know, *bonded* over her bruised knees or something. And then, when we were eight, there was that picture of her in the newspaper, wearing that miniature pink Jackie O suit. You said, 'She's going to be my girlfriend someday,' and then you cut that picture out and put it in your little Velcro wallet and kept it there until it practically disintegrated."

"None of that ever happened!"

"How can you not remember that? Hey, I understand you forgetting the time we were four—I have trouble remembering much from when we were really little too—but the other?"

"I remember the Velcro wallet . . ." It had a Superman insignia on it.

And suddenly, the memories come crashing in. Everything Sandy is saying—it's all true.

"How did I never remember this before?" I ask, stunned.

"I don't know." Sandy shrugs. "Maybe when you saw her again, all grown up, your mind refused to make a connection to the past, because the person you were seeing in front of you was the daughter of your mom's political enemy and you weren't *supposed* to like her?"

Seriously? All along, I've been a party loyalist?

Another shrug from Sandy. "The mind's a funny thing. But I do know one thing."

"Which is?"

"Katie Willfield, from the time you were small, has *always* been the girl for you."

I'm still trying to digest all this when Sandy continues with, "I don't know what I was thinking—I swear I wasn't trying to break you up—but before I knew it, I'd posted the pictures. And then, when you said you and she were hitting the campaign trail together, I figured everything was fine between you. But now I come to find out that you broke up and part of the reason is me . . ."

I'm just dumbstruck, taking it all in.

"You should have told me the truth from the beginning!" Sandy says painfully.

"I didn't think I could trust you with it," I say. "And obviously, I was right."

"But you weren't! Because, if you had trusted me? If you had *told* me not to say or do something, I wouldn't have—hey, I'm educable!"

Something about the way he says that last part—so SAT-prep word—makes me start to laugh. Soon, Sandy's laughing too. Still, our laughter has a sad, trailing quality to it.

"You still like her," Sandy says into the silence that follows our outburst.

As soon as he says this, I realize it's true.

"Yes, but—"

"Don't tell me again how she betrayed you, and even if she didn't, it wouldn't matter because she's mad at you about the pics. Which we both know now is all my fault."

Who needs to say anything when you have a best friend to do your talking for you?

In the end, I simply nod.

"I don't know how I'm going to do it yet," Sandy says, "but somehow I'm going to make it up to you."

KATIE

The morning following the final debate, Kent and I are parked outside of Drew's hotel, waiting for him. But when the opposite passenger side door of the limo opens, it's not Drew who slides in. Instead, it's some boy I've never seen before in T-shirt and jeans. I'm about to scream for help—*Who is this guy?*—when Drew slides in after him, shuts the door.

The guy holds out his hand to me. "Hey, what's up?"

Reluctantly, I shake his hand and crane my neck around him to eyeball Drew. "Friend of yours?" I say.

"This is Sandy," Drew says, "my best friend from home. My mom flew him in. She thought it would be a good idea to have him spend the day with us."

At first, I'm appalled. But then I think: Why not? This is Drew's and my last day together. This is the last time we'll have to publicly maintain our charade, because after today we'll go back to campaigning with our respective parents and then it's just one short week until the election. Then this will all be over with. So why not have Sandy here? Maybe he'll act as a buffer. Maybe with him here, it'll be less awkward and we can just get this final homestretch over with.

"Yo." Sandy reaches a hand over to the front seat. "Kent, right? Heard a lot about you."

After shaking Kent's hand, Sandy settles back, stretches his arms wide against the back of the seat, and puts an arm around Drew's and my shoulders, giving us a squeeze. "So, kids. What've we got planned for today?"

I pull out my clipboard. "Well, first I was thinking—"

"Let me see that," Sandy says.

He takes the clipboard from me and starts reading the items out loud. When he's done, he says, "Yeah. No. We're not doing any of that," and hands the clipboard back to me.

Okay, I know he's Drew's best friend, but seriously, who *is* this guy?

"Then what are we doing?" I finally ask.

Sandy leans back, digging one hand into a tight jeans pocket and removing a piece of paper. After unfolding the many folds, he tries to iron it out with a palm on his knee. "I've got my own list," he says proudly.

"May I see that?" I extend my hand for the crumpled mess.

"Um, no," Sandy says. Then he leans over the seat again, points to a place on the page to Kent. "Yo, Kent. Can you find this spot?"

With Sandy still leaning forward, I have a clear view of Drew. I mouth at him: *Where's he taking us?*

But Drew just shrugs back at me, helpless, like: What's a guy supposed to do?

You would think that being from Connecticut, wealthy, and a girl—not necessarily in that order!—would make me inclined to love horses. Well, I'm here to tell you, such is not the case. It's not that I dislike horses, but I'm on the short side, I've never had the chance to ride before—too busy furthering my father's political career—and, I'm a control freak. Even at the dentist's office, I prefer to keep one foot on the floor. Also:

"A spider!"

I did mention that spiders represent the third greatest fear of humans, right?

Only it's more than just an Eek, a spider! moment. This is the biggest, hairiest spider I've ever seen in my life, moseying its way across the desert floor.

The desert. For riding. Yes, this is the first stop on the magical mystery tour that Sandy is taking us on.

Sandy cocks his head at the tarantula, squinting one eye shut. "I'd say that's a good argument for just getting on the horse, Katie."

When he puts it like that, he doesn't have to ask me twice.

But getting up on the horse—short girl? tall horse?—takes a combination of Drew pushing and Sandy pulling.

"Now what do we do?" I ask, once Drew and Sandy are on their horses too.

"I don't know." Sandy shrugs, looks at Drew. "You know how to ride?"

"No."

"Me neither."

"Then *what* are we doing here?" I put in.

"I've always wanted to try it," Sandy says.

Drew shrugs. "I can think of worse things to do."

They click their heels against their horses' flanks and they're off at a slow pace.

"Shouldn't we have a guide?" I shout after them.

They fail to turn around.

"No, really!" I shout, a little more desperate now. "Shouldn't we have a guide?"

Still not turning around.

This really is the Wild West.

Thankfully the horses are old, and by doing what Sandy and Drew do, I'm able to follow.

When we return to the barn we got the horses from, an hour and a half later, I'm saddle sore and still brushing desert off my jeans from the two times I fell off. I'm also still laughing—at myself, us, at the absurdity of the whole situation.

Sandy holds the reins of my horse as I dismount.

"I think I fall better," I say, still laughing.

"She's a good sport," Sandy says to Drew. "You should keep her."

As Sandy leads the horses away, I mouth at Drew: Doesn't he know we're just faking?

But Drew just shrugs.

It's a big day for shrugging.

· · ·

And it's a big day for doing whatever Sandy wants us to do too.

The guy's got a whole plan. He takes us sightseeing various places, has us stop regularly for meals, and takes pictures of us everywhere we go with his iPhone. "For your adoring public, right?" he says.

And all the while, he keeps up a steady stream of chatter. If there's one thing Sandy can do, it's talk. He talks to me a lot and he talks to Drew a lot. Drew and me talking to each other, though? Not so much. But it doesn't seem to matter because Sandy's got us covered. Truth to tell, when he talks to me, I kind of like it. He's funny and interesting and—shocker!—he appears to think the same of me. At one point, he even says, "You're not half bad . . . for a Republican," which I take is a huge compliment coming from him. If anything, though, I like it most when he talks to Drew. Then I can just sit back and watch the glory of two people who know each other so well that they can tease each other mercilessly and still manage to have the love shine through. Best friends.

I have to say, I'm envious of that.

It's getting late in the day. The sky is beginning to change.

"Much as I hate to admit it," I say, "all good things must come to an end. Time to head back?"

Sandy pulls out his now familiar crumpled itinerary.

"Nah," he says. "How about one more stop?" Then: "Yo, Kent. Can you take us to the outskirts of town?"

· · ·

The outskirts of town. It sounds like something you'd hear in a Western. Or maybe a romance.

Funny, there are a whole bunch of other people hanging out on the outskirts of town.

"What's everyone here for?" I ask. "What's the big attraction?"

"Only that." Sandy points.

And that's when I see it: the sun setting over the city of Tucson, a whole array of amazing colors trailing across the sky. I watch, we all do, until the sun disappears entirely.

It's so beautiful.

"I guess we go now?" I say with a sigh.

"No," Sandy says. "Now we wait."

"For?"

If I've learned one thing today, though, it's that there's not much point in arguing with Sandy. So I wait, and surprisingly, all the other people on the outskirts of town wait too, staring up at the sky. Maybe they know something I don't?

With the sun gone, the sky gradually darkens. And as it does, stars begin to wink, slowly at first and then so rapidly until there are more stars in the sky than I've ever seen in my life.

"Pretty amazing, huh?" Sandy says, sounding pleased with himself. Well, who can blame him?

"It's like being in an observatory," I admit, "but you don't need a telescope."

"Okay, great," Sandy says, his voice turning all businesslike, as he proceeds to instruct Drew, "now kiss her."

"*What?*" we both cry.

Well, at least we finally agree on one thing.

"Go on." Sandy pulls out his iPhone, holds it in our direction to frame the shot. "Kiss her."

"Didn't you tell him . . .?" I start to hiss at Drew. Then quickly, I look around us to see if anyone's heard, but everyone else is too busy staring at the stars. "That we're not together anymore?"

"I told him," Drew says, with a shrug like: But what do you expect? The guy's crazy.

"Yeah, yeah, I know all that," Sandy says. "But all those other pictures you've been taking of yourselves as a couple— sightseeing this, sightseeing that, *occasionally* with your arms around each other—it's all nice and stuff. But don't you think all your fans out there would like to see something *real*? You know, one of the guy kissing the girl?"

I don't know what comes over me, but I don't wait for Drew to decide what the right thing to do is. Instead I reach up, grab him by the T-shirt with both fists, pull his face toward mine, and plant my lips on his before he can resist.

As Drew slides his arms around my waist to pull me closer, for the briefest of minutes while we perform just for the camera, I feel like something's been righted in my world. How I've missed this: the feeling of his body pressed next to mine, the feeling that *he* is mine. And oh, how I miss those kisses. How I wish things still were the way they used to be, when we kissed not for the cameras, but just for us.

So caught up am I in longing for the person who's right next to me, I'm only vaguely aware of the sound of the camera clicking:

Snick.

Snick.

I've heard that sound before.

DREW

Election night.

Yes, it's finally here.

The first returns are scheduled to come in at seven, with Georgia, Indiana, Kentucky, South Carolina, Vermont, and Virginia reporting, and we're all gathered in our hotel in Hartford. My mom, Dad, the twins, Clint, Ann, and all the staffers who can cram into the penthouse suite. My mom wanted to watch from home, but Ann said it would be better to do it from Connecticut's capital city, so we could use the ballroom downstairs when the final results are in. As it happens, the Willfield campaign has made the same choice. Only they're installed in the hotel across the street.

You need two hundred and seventy of the electoral votes to win a presidential election in the United States. Two hundred and seventy—that's the magic number. If my mom reaches that, we'll go down to the ballroom for the most hectic party ever and thousands upon thousands of red, white, and blue balloons will be released from nets hanging from the rafters. If she loses? The balloons will stay in their nets and it will be a much more sober affair as she gives her concession speech.

Even though it's just six, with those first returns still an hour away, we're already glued to the TV. Who knew that finding out who the next Leader of the Free World is going to be could be so fascinating? I didn't. But I do now.

Which is why it takes me a minute to realize that my iPhone is vibrating against my leg.

When I pick it up, I see it's a text from Sandy.

It's funny. In a way, back at the Democratic Primary celebration, this all began with a text from Sandy, so it's somehow fitting that it should end this way too. I read what he's written:

It was never her.

I type back: What r u talking about?

Him: Katie.

Me: What?

Him: Thing @ ur dad.

Me: What???

Him: Watch TV. Soon every1'll know.

I have no idea what he's talking about, but I look up at the TV screen and sure enough, there's a special bulletin crawling across the bottom of the screen. Can it be some of the returns already? But no. I look at the countdown clock and that's still a ways away. So I look back at the special bulletin to see the final words of it: . . . from the Treadwell campaign. What is this? But no sooner does the crawl end than the talking heads start talking about what this is.

"This just in," one of the election analysts says. "It has been discovered that the unconfirmed source of a story a few weeks back—that Samantha Reilly's husband was cheating on her— was in fact someone from the Treadwell campaign, fabricating the truth. It seems prudent to point out that this new development has been confirmed."

Another one of the analysts chuckles at this. "So I guess it turns out that Mr. Clean Campaign was the real dirty player? Not that it will hurt him any. His campaign was already over with."

Which is true. The debates clearly showed the voters what a whack job Bix Treadwell is, and in this last week my mom and Katie's dad have broken way ahead of him in the polls. Although they're still neck and neck with each other.

And then all the analysts chuckle. Really? This is a chuckle moment? My family is hurt, my father's good name is smeared, and my romance with Katie destroyed by false rumor . . . and they think it's funny? What a bunch of clowns.

And then it hits me: Sandy knew about this story before it broke. My iPhone starts to vibrate again.

I pick it up to see just one word there:

Well?

You wouldn't think a single word followed by a question mark could be smug, but there you go.

The look on my face as I stare at my phone—if I could just be outside myself right now, I imagine I'd see something on the level of horror-film incredulity.

Me: You knew about this in advance.
Him: I have my ways.

But how?

Me: YOU did this?
Him: Again, I have my ways.

I don't know what to say to this, but I don't have to as Sandy gets the last word:

Now, go get the girl.

But I can't do that, can I? What am I going to say to her? Oh, I didn't believe you when you were telling the truth, but now that everyone else knows the truth I believe you so can we maybe go on from here?

Yeah, right. Like that's going to work.

But then I think: I have to at least try. That's the thing about everything in life, from the smallest things you want to romance and even presidential elections:

You can never know the outcome in advance, but at the very least, you have to try.

"Can you believe that guy?" my dad is saying to the screen.

They must be talking about the Bix Treadwell revelation.

"That's politics," my mom says. It surprises me, the lack of anger in her voice. She seems to accept it as being just another part of the game. I suppose she's used to it. I'm not sure I'll ever be.

I pick up my iPhone to get in touch with Kat—I'm already thinking of her as Kat again—and it occurs to me: after all this time, I don't even have her number.

I get up off the sofa, grab my coat on the way to the door.

"Drew?" my mom calls. "The results will start coming in soon. Where are you going?"

"There's something I've got to take care of," I shout from the doorway, "but I'll be back!" Then I walk back and give her a quick kiss on the forehead and whisper, "You're going to do great, Mom. Whatever happens, you're going to do great."

And I'm gone.

You'd think it'd be easier to get in to see someone at a hotel.

After crossing the street and going through the revolving doors, I approach the clerk at the front desk and ask what suite Katie Willfield and her party is staying in, only to be met with:

"I'm sorry, sir, but we're not at liberty to give out that information."

"You don't understand," I say. "We're friends."

"Yes," he says, "that's the line all the young men use."

Other young men? Other guys have been trying to get up to see her?

"But I'm her boyfriend," I say.

Well, I was. And anyway, almost no one in the country knows I'm not anymore, so . . .

"Riiiiight," the clerk says. "And I'm the Queen of England."

"Don't you recognize me?" I point at my face but he looks at me blankly. "Never mind."

I head for the bank of elevators.

If he won't tell me what suite she's in, I'll find her myself.

"Where do you think you're going?" the clerk shouts after me, his previous snooty tone now replaced with desperation. Then, when I don't respond: "Security!"

Before I know it, two burly security guards have me by the armpits, dragging me backward through the lobby. As I'm being dragged, I see Kent watching from the elevator bank in bemusement.

"Kent!" I shout. "You know me! Let me up to the suite!"

"I can't do that," he says. "But if you wait outside, I'll tell her you're here."

With that, I'm thrust back out through the doors and onto the street.

And *that's* how you get thrown out of a hotel.

I wait outside in the cold for what seems like forever, pacing the pavement, using my time to rehearse what I'm going to say. What if she doesn't come? And if she does, what good is a rehearsed statement? I'm not making up fake campaign promises here, trying to earn votes. This is real.

I'll just speak from what's in my heart.

"Drew?"

I turn, and then there she is, coming through the revolving doors, holding her arms across her chest as she shivers against the cold.

"Hey," I say, trying on a joke as she approaches, "didn't you read the *Farmer's Almanac*? They said it was going to be cold tonight, maybe even snow."

But she ignores my lame attempt at humor. "What's this all about?" she says. "I need to get back upstairs."

"Yeah, okay, listen."

But I can't stand to see her shivering like that, so I take off my coat. "Here," I say, draping it around her shoulders.

It's worth noting that she doesn't say thank you, just continues looking at me, hard. "Well?" she says when I fail to speak. "I'm listening."

It's now or never. I take a deep breath and start to speak.

"I know now that it wasn't you behind the rumor about my dad and—"

"Right," she cuts me off. "You know, because the world knows, it was Bix. So, thanks for the apology and all . . ." She starts to turn away.

"That's not it!" I call after her.

She turns. "Then what is?"

"Look, I already had this discussion, in my head." I point at my head to demonstrate, and feeling foolish, put my hand down. "I know it's not enough for me to say, Oops, my mistake! It wasn't you. Can we go on from here?"

"You want to . . . go on from here?"

"Yes! But here's the thing: It shouldn't have mattered who was behind the story, Bix or any other person. The important thing is that I should have listened to you when you first said it wasn't you. I should have trusted your word. Just like I should have trusted in my dad and Sandy."

She looks puzzled at this last part. If I get the time later, which I hope I will, I'll explain everything.

"But most of all," I continue, "I should have trusted *you*. If you're going to choose to have a person in your life, if you fall in love with someone, you have to also choose to trust that person. Because if you don't have that, if you're not going to trust the most important people in your life, then what do you have?"

"You're . . . in love with me?"

"I think I always have been," I say. And then, as she stares at me with increasing wonder, I proceed to tell her about all that Sandy reminded me of: how we met when we were four, how I carried her picture in my wallet when we were eight.

There's astonishment in her eyes as she says, "I *remember* that boy. I *remember* that day at the summer festival."

I love that astonishment in her eyes. I love everything about her eyes. I love *her*.

"It's always been you, Kat," I say.

"Drew . . ."

I see a single snowflake settle on her hair, followed by a few more.

"What do you know?" I hold my arms out wide. "The *Farmer's Almanac* is right again!"

"It can't work," she says and I feel the smile immediately disappear from my face.

"You don't love me back?"

"No. I mean, yes, I do—love you, that is, but—"

"Kat," I say, "is it that you still think I was responsible for leaking those photos from the night of the masquerade ball because—"

"I know it wasn't you."

"Because you trusted me?"

Is this what's going to kill my chances, that she was smart enough to trust me while I was stupid enough not to believe her?

"No," she says. "But I should have. It was Sandy."

"How do you know that?"

"Because he told me. In Arizona."

"When?"

"You were in the bathroom or something, and he confessed that it was him. And he confessed about why he did it."

"Why didn't you say anything?"

She doesn't answer this. Instead she says, "I made him promise not to tell you I knew. Because what would be the point? You still thought I was behind the story about your dad."

Sandy kept his promise to her? What a time for the dude to keep silent!

"You know," she says, "you're lucky to have him for a friend."

I realize that it's true: I am lucky to have Sandy.

"But if you know the truth now," I say, "and I know the truth, then why can't this work?"

"Drew," she says, "in a few hours, either your mom or my father is going to be elected president of the United States. And then, in January, one of us will move to Washington, DC to live in the White House. How can we make a relationship work with all that?"

It gives me hope that she uses the word "relationship" and not "romance." Romances, they can be such temporary things. You fall for someone in the cafeteria line at school on Monday and before the Friday pep rally, it's all over. But a relationship, that's something that sounds like it could have a future in it. That sounds like something that, if two people are incredibly lucky, could go on and on.

With no shortage of romance in it, of course.

"I don't have all the answers, Kat. I don't even have most of them." I put my hands in her hair. The snow is falling harder now. "But if two people love each other like I love you and you love me . . ."

I look at her questioningly and she nods, confirming that she loves me back.

"Then," I say, "if there's one thing I've learned in the past few months it's that, at the very least, you have to try. *We* have to try."

For the first time since she came out here, her mouth tilts into a smile.

I love that smile.

And seeing it, I do what I've wanted to do for what seems like forever. I lower my face to hers and kiss her, and she kisses me back.

A roar goes up and at first I'm confused. Is someone cheering for us? And then I realize what it must be—the election returns are beginning to come in.

In a few moments, we'll have to go our separate ways and wait to see how this all turns out. But after that? Who knows? Like I said, I don't have all the answers. In fact, I have hardly any.

But as the snow falls more steadily and more cheers go up, I kiss her again, harder, a promise for the future. And as she kisses me back just as hard, I can't help but be filled with hope.

It's starting.

ACKNOWLEDGMENTS

Thanks to Pamela Harty, for friendship above all else, and to everyone at The Knight Agency.

Thanks to Laura Whitaker, for stepping in with precision and verve, and to Sarah Shumway and everyone at Bloomsbury.

Thanks to the Friday Night Irregulars: Lauren Catherine, Bob Gulian, Andrea Schicke Hirsch, and Greg Logsted (who doubles as my husband).

Thanks to Backspace for being a terrific site for writers and BookBalloon for being a terrific site for readers.

Thanks to booksellers and librarians for years of support, and Twitter and FB for years of diversion.

Thanks to readers everywhere, my favorite of whom is my daughter, Jackie, who's all-around terrific even when she's not reading.

Lauren Baratz-Logsted is the author of more than twenty books for adults, teens, and young readers, including *Little Women and Me*, *The Twin's Daughter*, *Crazy Beautiful*, and the Sisters 8 series, which she cowrites with her husband and daughter.

www.laurenbaratzlogsted.com
@LaurenBaratzL

An hour later, I'm huffing and puffing as I lean in, my hands gripping the carved wooden armrest as I shove, hard, on the couch. It moves only an inch.

An inch.

Stupid freakin' behemoth couch. I feel like I'm trying to move a Mack truck. Trees must have weighed more in the seventeenth century.

Yeah, that makes sense.

I groan and push again, straining with all my might. The leg screeches against the marble floors and then gives way, sliding abruptly. My hands slip off the armrest, and I slam to the ground.

"Oomph," I say, my forehead resting on the cool floor that had, moments ago, been covered by a French provincial sofa.

The ground is musty. Dusty. Like, oh, I don't know, it's been covered by a couch for a few decades. I've gotten so used to the polished-until-I-can-see-my-reflection cleanliness in this place that it's almost foreign to smell actual dirt.

Footsteps shuffle closer, and I suddenly realize I'm not alone. Crap, I hope my mom isn't going to bust me. . . .

I roll over and look up into the amused, warm brown eyes of a boy close to my age. He's leaning over, resting his hands on his knees as he peers down. I blink as if he's a mirage and he'll disappear. Spotting a guy like him in a place like this is harder than finding a lifeboat on the *Titanic*.

But he doesn't.

Disappear, that is.

Awesome. The first boy under seventy I've seen in this place, and he finds me lying facedown on the floor of the billiards room.

"It was the candlestick," I say abruptly, because it's the only thing I can think of and I'm fighting the urge to check him out.

He's cute. Really, really cute. He looks . . . Costa Rican. Maybe part Native American or part African American . . . or some combination uniquely his, because I've never seen a guy so totally drool worthy.

In a place like this, a place filled with rich, elderly white people, he stands out, dazzling in a way that has nothing to do with race, and everything to do with . . .

I blink, realizing that while I've been staring, his lips have been moving.

". . . was the sofa?" he asks, furrowing his brow as he walks around so that he can face me as I sit up.

"Oh, uh, no, the sofa's a little too heavy to use as a weapon. It was definitely the candlestick," I say, and then jut my thumb in the direction of an antique brass candelabrum. "And Professor Plum. Because he's weird-looking and I don't trust him."

One side of his mouth curls up as he reaches out to me.

I study him for a second before finally reaching out to accept his hand. It's warm and soft and strong, and he easily pulls me to my feet. And then I'm standing close to him. So close I can smell him.

Cinnamon. I breathe deeper, enjoying the warm spiciness of it. Yes, he smells like cinnamon. As I rake in another breath, I catch him staring.

Abruptly I step away, realizing I'm standing within inches of him, just breathing him in over and over like an idiot.

"Ahhh," he says, once he has room to talk without speaking directly into my ear. "Because we're in the billiards room, of course."

"Yeah," I say, suddenly realizing how lame and outdated my joke is. Maybe if I didn't play board games with old people all the time…

To avoid looking at him, I dust off the seat of my pants and focus *really hard* on my apron.

Oh god. I'm wearing a doily apron in front of a hot boy. "I always pegged it on Mrs. Peacock," he says.

"Oh?" I ask, wondering if there's a way to ditch the apron without looking like it's because of him. I glance around, but it's not like there's a phone booth where I can go from the bumbling Clark Kent to the ultra-suave Superman. I don't even have a pair of glasses to take off. "Why's that?"

"She's the only one not named after a color."

I furrow my brow. "That's not true. Peacock is a color."

"Are you sure?" he asks, crossing his arms. I'm suddenly, acutely aware of how built this boy is. He has serious muscles. Glorious, beautiful muscles, evident even through his stark white button-down and perfectly tailored black vest. He looks like he just left a wedding reception and lost his jacket somewhere.

"Yeah, it's a shade of blue. All the characters in Clue are colors," I say, realizing in some corner of my mind that's still functioning that I should probably shut up about Clue.

"I'll have to take your word for it," he says, flashing a cocky grin. He reaches out toward my face, and I freeze, half-expecting him to caress my cheek like something from a romance novel. But he doesn't. Instead he touches my hair, then pulls his hand away.

The way he looks at me, amusement glimmering in his eyes as he turns his hand and reveals a dust bunny, it's like he *knew* what he was doing. Like he knew I'd think he was reaching out for ... some other reason. And I fell for it.

Sheesh, I am so totally deprived of flirting-with-a-cute-guy opportunities, living in a retirement home with my mom. I need to get out more. I need to get a hobby or something before I swoon at his feet and ask if he wants to play bridge.

He smirks. "Sorry, it was kind of clinging to your ponytail. It was distracting."

"Well, I find your hair distracting too," I say, and then immediately wish I had just kept my trap shut.

I find your hair distracting? That was the best I could do?

"Really," he says, his eyebrow quirking. I'm suddenly, acutely aware that his eyebrows are better groomed than mine.

One of them, the right one, has two slashes through it, like he had it trimmed that way. Like he had them ... sculpted to match the lines where his hair is buzzed shorter and little lines swoop and twirl on the sides of his head.

And I'm wearing an apron made of doilies.

"Yeah," I say, my face warming. "Your haircut is, um, crooked."

He smiles, that same amusement as earlier glittering in his eyes. "It's *supposed* to be crooked."

My laughter sounds like a barking seal having seizures, and I can't believe he doesn't back away. Instead, his eyes light up.